Her Secret

Not all secrets are kept

Alyssa DiSanza

Ukiyoto Publishing

All global publishing rights are held by

Ukiyoto Publishing

Published in 2020

Content Copyright © **Alyssa DiSanza**

ISBN 9789359209647

All rights reserved.

No part of this publication may be reproduced, transmitted, or stored in a retrieval system, in any form by any means, electronic, mechanical, photocopying, recording or otherwise, without the prior permission of the publisher.

The moral rights of the author have been asserted.

This is a work of fiction. Names, characters, businesses, places, events, locales, and incidents are either the products of the author's imagination or used in a fictitious manner. Any resemblance to actual persons, living or dead, or actual events is purely coincidental.

This book is sold subject to the condition that it shall not by way of trade or otherwise, be lent, resold, hired out or otherwise circulated, without the publisher's prior consent, in any form of binding or cover other than that in which it is published.

CONTENTS

Chapter One	*1*
Chapter Two	*4*
Chapter Three	*7*
Chapter Four	*10*
Chapter Five	*13*
Chapter Six	*16*
Chapter Seven	*20*
Chapter Eight	*24*
Chapter Nine	*28*
Chapter Ten	*33*
Chapter Eleven	*36*
Chapter Twelve	*41*
Chapter Thirteen	*46*
Chapter Fourteen	*50*
Chapter Fifteen	*54*
Chapter Sixteen	*57*
Chapter Seventeen	*63*
Chapter Eighteen	*69*
Chapter Nineteen	*73*
Chapter Twenty	*79*
Chapter Twenty-One	*82*
Chapter Twenty-Two	*87*
Chapter Twenty-Three	*91*
Chapter Twenty-Four	*97*

Chapter Twenty-Five	103
Chapter Twenty-Six	111
Chapter Twenty-Seven	117
Chapter Twenty-Eight	123
Chapter Twenty-Nine	129
Chapter Thirty	134
Chapter Thirty-One	137
Chapter Thirty-Two	139
Epilogue	142
About the Author	**146**

Chapter One

ATHENA LEWIS

W AKING UP TO MY annoying alarm clock, I throw my warm blanket off myself and shiver as the cold air hits my warm body. When I get out of bed, I walk over to my closet and sigh before I pick out a light grey sweater and blue jeans. The first day back to school after winter break. *Yay!* Note the sarcasm.

This year's winter break was not very eventful for me, I worked, slept and ate. The only exciting thing was spending Christmas with my mother. I'm eighteen and in my senior year of high school. I just want to finish my senior year and bury my head in a book while drinking tea.

I plan to go to a community college for writing classes after graduation. My dream job is to be a published author. Just the thought of having my books published has that feeling of hope blossoming in my stomach.

When I finish getting ready, I run down the stairs. Hurrying so I won't be late, I throw on a pair of my converse. I say bye to my mom while walking out the door and in the direction of the school building.

When I make it to school, I quicken my pace, hoping I'm lucky to go unnoticed by all the popular teenagers. Not in the mood to deal with their shit, especially the Queen Bee, Emily's, shit.

But luck is not on my side. I groan as Emily and her posse notice me.

"Oh, look what the sewer dragged in," Emily sneers at me while everyone laughs. I roll my eyes. Seriously, that made no sense.

"Why would you say such rude things about yourself?" I sneer back at her, crossing my arms over my chest. "I guess your hair dye is getting to your brain."

"You'll be sorry, Athena!" Emily scoffs and walks off, her group of friends following after her.

I walk past the rest of the teenagers and head to my locker to grab my books for my first class, which is math. My shoes move against the tiled and shiny floor as I walk through the classroom door and take my usual seat in the back near the window, ignoring the gossip and giggles over the school's quarterback, Ezra Kingston.

I look out the window and lose myself in my thoughts, trying to avoid the hurtful words that came from Emily Colt.

Believe it or not, Emily and I used to be best friends. I started dating her twin brother Zeke in 8th grade up until Junior year. Emily and I practically became sisters over time. We did everything together when I wasn't spending time with Zeke.

Well, everything changed one icy winter night.

A hand pops up in front of my face, snapping me out of my thoughts. Looking up, I see Ms. Jane standing in front of me, Ezra Kingston standing next to her, a small smile playing on his pink lips that look as soft as clouds. *Fucking hell.*

"Ms. Lewis, Ezra is going to be sitting next to you from now on," she informs me, smiling. I nod as Ezra fucking Kingston plops his ass on the seat next to me with a smile and a notebook in hand. Girls start glaring daggers at me, jealousy practically flowing off them.

Thanks, Ms. Jane.

Ms. Jane walks up to the front of the classroom and starts her lesson. I zone out since I already read ahead over the break. I feel someone start poking me, but I ignore it and watch Ms. Jane point to things on the board.

Poke. *Stop*.

Poke. *Go away*.

Poke. *Leave*.

Poke. *That's it*.

Turning sharply towards him, I stare into Ezra's green eyes, glaring. It is only now in this moment that I notice the vibrant green in his eyes.

"May I borrow a pencil?" he whispers quietly. I scowl at him and get a pencil out of my bag for him.

I give it to him and our fingers brush against each others. He smiles and I turn my eyes back to Ms. Jane, flustered.

Chapter Two

ATHENA LEWIS

THROUGHOUT FIRST PERIOD, Ezra would not stop trying to talk to me. Every time I would look away from the board, I would see girls glaring at me. They should know it isn't my fault Ms. Jane ordered him to sit next to me.

Finally, the first period ended.

I start collecting my things as Emily comes up to me with her group of friends that used to be my friends. An irritated sigh leaves my lips. Waiting for her insults, I raise an eyebrow at her. She looks conflicted like she wants to say something else, however, she decides against it.

"God, you're such a nerd like who would even want you," she says, making the lingering students around us snicker. Consumed with anger, I let out a fake laugh, instead of punching her in the face that's looking very punchable at this given moment.

"You know, Emily, what happened wasn't my fault!" I shout at her. She seems taken aback by my outburst and looks at me with tears in her eyes along with regret. I scoff and walk past her to my next class English, the same class Ezra, unfortunately, attends.

When I get there, I sit down in my seat and zone out.

Lunch...

I've always hated it ever since I started getting bullied. I remember the first time I got a tray of food dumped on me. *Fun.*

Emily and her new best friend, Stacy decided it would be nice to dump scalding hot chili on me. I glance down at my arm where the scar from the chili is. What makes everything funny is that when Emily humiliates me, she has pain, regret and anger in her eyes. If only she knew. If only she would listen.

Sighing, I head towards the cafeteria and go in the direction of my table where me, myself, and I sit. As I take a seat, I pull out my laptop and begin writing down notes for the chapters of my book I'm in the process of making. I take a sip of my water and go back to typing.

I tune out and while typing, I see a shadow cast over me. I turn around and come face to face with Stacy but no Emily. *Oh no.*

"I don't even see why you write, it's not like it's any good, so I decided I would help you out." Stacy says with a smirk. My eyes widen at her statement.

I don't have time to move my laptop that I have worked so hard for as Stacy dumps her lunch all over me and my laptop. My heart plummets to the bottom of my stomach and anger starts to bubble within me. Everyone begins laughing and a tear of embarrassment and anger rolls down my cheek. Stacy flips her hair and struts away.

The only person who doesn't laugh is Ezra.

I glance back at my now goop covered laptop and pull out my hard drive. I thankfully remembered to put it in, to save my work if anything like that happens. I put everything besides my laptop in my bag and stand up. Ignoring the laughter, I begin walking towards the bathroom to clean everything off of it and myself.

When school ends, I waste no time in leaving. I ignore everyone, especially when Emily comes up to me sobbing. I just look at her and walk away.

I should be the one crying, not her. I'm the one who has to go through this shit everyday.

When I get home, I try my best to see if my laptop is working. I put it in rice and go to my room.

I fall on my bed and begin sobbing into my fluffy pillow. "Why me? It wasn't my fault! I wasn't the one that caused the crash that took him away from me!"

"Dear God, why me? What did I do to you? It wasn't my fault!" I shout at the ceiling of my room. "It wasn't my fault," I whisper, closing my eyes, readying myself for nightmares.

Chapter Three

ATHENA LEWIS

*S**ITTING IN THE car with Zeke, I glance over at him. I see him smiling, a happy expression on his face. I'm happy too. How could I not be? We created a life. Just then car lights come speeding towards us, blinding us for a moment.*

The blare of a car horn sounds through the air. All that's heard is the sound of metal bending, tires screeching along with glass shattering. I feel myself go upside down and my head jerks, hitting the cold window.

Fear flows through my body and my shaking hands wrap themselves around my stomach.

"Zeke, I love you!" I shout through the chaos. He looks over at me, tears streaming down his face. He glances at my stomach and places a hand on it.

"I-I love you too, sweetheart!" He manages to shout back as the car rolls. I hold his other hand, tightly, watching as everything blurs around us. Blood drips from Zeke's head as we stare at each other with fear in our eyes.

The car stops and all that's heard is my heartbeat and ringing in my ears. The smell of smoke and melted rubber lingering in the air. I look over at Zeke and see him pale, his chest not moving. He's not breathing. I begin sobbing while I try to unbuckle myself.

"Call 9-1-1!" A frantic voice shouts.

I manage to unbuckle myself, hissing in pain as I drop down, landing on the shattered glass. "Zeke, you can't leave me! Please you can't! I need you!" I shout as I try to reach him, going in and out of consciousness.

"I love you," I whisper as I hear sirens in the background. I feel myself get pulled out of the car and frantic yelling voices all around me. "My baby," I mumble, fearing that our baby didn't survive.

I pass out while my arms are wrapped protectively around my stomach.

My baby.

I shoot out of bed, panting and gasping for air. Sitting up, I throw the covers off of me with one thought running through my head.

Where is he?
Where is he?

Everything around me begins to blur and my breathing becomes irregular. I gasp for air, beads of sweat dripping down my forehead, and landing on my shirt.

I start clawing at my chest. Darkness invades my vision as I gasp and fight for air. I try to look around my room for things to name. Black starts dotting my vision even more and I slump against my headboard and let the darkness overtake me.

Where is he?
Where is he?

Chapter Four

EMILY COLT

EVERY TIME I HUMILIATE Athena, I don't only hurt her, but also myself. We were best friends. Two peas in a pod. But after Zeke died I was filled with anger. I slapped her one day because I couldn't stand looking at her.

She was a reminder of my brother. She got to say goodbye and I didn't. I hated her for that. But I regret everything now because if Zeke was here he would kill me for treating her like I am. I hate myself for it.

I want my best friend back and I will try my damned hardest to make up for everything.

ATHENA LEWIS

I wake up to the sound of my mom knocking on my door, "Sweetie, wake up. It's time for dinner," my mother, Rhea, calls out from the other side of my wooden door.

"Okay, mom. I'll be right there, but I need to take a shower," I respond while crawling out of bed.

"Don't take too long," she replies, her footsteps walking away from my door.

I walk over to my bathroom that's connected to my room and get in the shower. I turn the water on and strip out of my sweaty clothes. I step into the path of the water and gasp as the warm water hits my body. I tilt my head down and stare at the drain, watching the water swirl down it.

I get lost in my thoughts, thinking about my nightmare and son. I have to finish off the school year without complications and then I can go get my son from his temporary adoptive family. I visit him whenever I'm not at school or working.

His name is Ian and he is seven months old. I named him after Zeke since Ian was his middle name. Ian looks so much like him, brown hair and blue eyes. Nobody except my mom knows about him, not even Zeke's family. They all turned against me and cut all ties when he passed away. I could never inform them that I was pregnant, so I gave up on stressing myself out and trying to get a hold of them.

It wasn't my fault. But I guess they blame me since I'm the only one that survived. The driver from the other car died on impact and she was highly intoxicated. I left Seattle for a year and went to Ohio for therapy, to help with my depression after losing the love of my life and to keep my pregnancy a secret.

When I returned from Ohio, I placed Ian with a temporary adoptive family. I'm keeping him there until I graduate so I can move away.

Turning the water off, I step out of the shower and wrap a fluffy blue towel around my body. Blue is my favorite color. I love everything about it. Light blue is calm and dark blue is sort of depressing and sad.

I walk into my room and get changed into comfy clothes. I walk downstairs and see my mom setting the food on the table. I walk up to her and kiss her on the cheek. I give her a small hug. She and I are pretty close. She was disappointed when I told her I was pregnant, but she eventually came around.

"Hey, mom," I mumble, still hugging her.

"Hi, sweetie," she replies, rubbing my back. "Did you have another nightmare?" She questions with concern and I nod against her shoulder.

"Yes, and I had a panic attack. Mom, I couldn't calm down. How am I supposed to take care of Ian after I graduate if I can't even get my life on track? I feel so helpless," I sob and bury my face in her straight black hair as her brown eyes well up with tears.

"Sweetie, maybe you should go back to seeing your therapist?" She reasons with me.

"Yeah, mom, I will. Could you give Dr. Barnes a call?" I ask her while pulling away from the hug. She nods and sits down. I take a seat across from her and wipe away my tears and begin eating dinner.

Chapter Five

ATHENA LEWIS

"HOW IS SCHOOL going, sweetheart?" My mom asks, taking a bite from her Caesar salad. I look over at her and frown, thinking about all the bullying.

"Not so good mom, Emily still hates me, and Stacy dumped her lunch on my laptop today," I tell her, picking at my food. My mom frowns as she places her hand on mine.

"Sweetheart, I'm so sorry that they are hurting you. It wasn't your fault, but when you graduate you can get Ian and we will move away, okay?" A couple of tears rolling down her cheek while she speaks.

"Okay, mom," I whisper, wiping away my tears. I continue eating my food as my mom tells me about the cooking show she has been watching. We share a few laughs and talk about dad.

My father passed away when I was around five years old. I still have bits and pieces of memories, but I have started to forget them over the years. I was a daddy's girl, but I still love both my parents. My father died in a car crash with me in it. I survived and I still blame myself for it. I survived and he didn't.

I had a fear of cars until Zeke came along. He helped me get over the fear and we eventually became best friends and then started dating. But I lost him the same way I lost my father. I'm terrified of cars because I lost two out of the four people I love the most, so I walk wherever I want to go.

"Remember when your dad dressed up as a princess to match with you on your fourth Halloween?" My mom asks, chuckling at the memory. I laugh with her, remembering the faint memories.

"I do, mom. He got so many weird looks from little girls and their families," I respond, giggling.

When I finish my dinner, I take my plate to the sink and then put it in the dishwasher.

"Thank you, mom," I say as I walk back into the dining room and kiss her forehead. She smiles, her blue eyes shining in the lights above us.

"You're welcome, sweetie. Sleep well," she says, standing up to hug me. I hug her back and kiss her forehead. "I'm going to call your therapist and schedule an appointment."

"Okay, thank you."

I pull away and head towards the stairs. Once I get to my room, I walk over to my desk and do some of my homework. Ms. Jane assigned us a paper that's filled with hard math problems to solve. *Like who knows how to do the math?* Not me.

Once I finish my math homework, I decide to work on a new chapter of my book, *The Fire Wolf*. It's a werewolf book that I'm in the process of writing. The female lead is a werewolf of course, but the exciting part is that she has the ability to control the element of fire.

While working for a couple of hours, I start feeling tired so I decide to finish up the paragraph and go to sleep. Once I'm changed into my night clothes, I go downstairs and grab my laptop to see if it still works. I power it on and it turns on, thank God.

I put it on my desk and plug it in. I put all of my school work in my bookbag and head towards the bathroom. After I brush my teeth, I turn off my lights and crawl into bed, slowly falling asleep when my head hits my soft pillow.

Chapter Six

ATHENA LEWIS

I WALK THROUGH the school doors the next morning with the usual frown on my face. I ignore everyone and walk to my locker.

When I get to my locker, I put in my combination and open it. I put my bag in and grab the only books I need for math. I place my head on the cool metal door and look down the hallway.

I stand there in shock when I see Emily give me a small and friendly smile. I snap myself out of my shocked state and roll my eyes at her. I see her smile fall into a frown. I slam the locker door shut and walk to my first class.

When I get to my first-period class, I sit down and stare out the window, waiting for Ms. Jane to start the class.

Ezra walks into the classroom and sits on the seat next to me. He gives me a charming smile when he looks over at me.

I manage to give him a half-smile. I rarely smile anymore, never finding a reason to.

"How has your day been?" He asks while placing his elbow on the table and resting his head against his palm.

"It's literally morning," I deadpan, making him frown. "But it's been okay," I add, feeling slightly guilty. He nods, looking at me with a small smile.

He looks at me expectantly. "Mine has been great, thanks for asking."

"Good for you," I reply harsher than intended. His smile falters and I sigh. "Sorry."

"It's alright."

That's where our conversation ends.

The rest of the class drags by slowly and soon enough the bell rings. I grab my things and make a quick stop at my locker to grab my books and my laptop for English class. Unfortunately, Ezra is also in this class.

Apparently, we have an essay due in two months, and Mr. Wilson is assigning our partners for it today.

"When I call your names go sit by your partner," he instructs, boredom in his tone.

"Mark and Jeremy."

"Stella and Brad."

"Aiden and Gianna."

I zone out until I hear my name.

"-thena and Ezra." *Are you fucking kidding me? Come on!*

Ezra smiles and walks over to me. "Hello again, *Sunshine*."

"Sunshine?" I ask in confusion and annoyance.

"It's my nickname for you now," Ezra clarifies and I roll my eyes.

"Ezra and Athena. Your topic is going to be The Effects of Pollution," Mr. Wilson informs us as he reads off of his wooden clipboard, flipping through multiple papers.

"That sounds easy enough," I mumble to myself.

"Yes, it does," Ezra agrees. I send him a look and then start researching the topic on my laptop.

I read through several articles and take notes while Ezra does the same. When I'm satisfied with the number of notes I took today, I pull out my book and start reading.

I glance over at Ezra who has his head resting against his palm while he clicks through articles on his computer. I almost smile at how sort of adorable he looks.

"Why are you staring, Sunshine?" Ezra asks while turning his head to look at me.

"I wasn't," I deny. "And I hate that nickname," I say while narrowing my eyes at him.

He smiles innocently at me then grins. "I know."

He turns back to his computer, completely ignoring my glare.

I hate that nickname so much.

Little does Athena know she really likes it deep down.

Chapter Seven

ATHENA LEWIS

"AM I COMING over your house or are you coming over mine for the essay?" Ezra asks me as we walk out of the loud classroom.

"Um, I don't know. It's up to you."

"Well, I guess I'll come over yours."

"Okay," I reply simply, walking down the crowded hall with Ezra by my side.

"Can I have your phone number, Sunshine?" Ezra asks. "You know just to discuss the essay arrangements."

With a nod, I dig my phone out of my tight jean pocket and give it to him. "Here."

He puts his contact in and gives me my phone back. I look at the contact name and sigh in relief that he just put his name and not something like *Daddy Ezra* or something like that.

"Bye, Sunshine," Ezra smiles, starting to walk away.

"Bye, Ezra," I smile back, raising my hand to give him a small wave.

I walk down the hallway towards my locker to get my other books for my third class, which is History.

History goes by in a breeze and I walk out of the classroom with a sigh of relief. My history teacher makes me want to punch him. He is a cranky old man and gives out detentions like they're candy.

I make my way down the crammed hall towards my locker. I slow my pace when I see the one and only Emily Colt standing right next to my locker.

I open my locker and completely ignore her presence. After placing my heavy ass books in my locker, I slam it closed and start walking away.

Emily grabs my arm, her manicured fingernails sharp against my skin and turns me towards her.

"Can I fucking help you?" I ask her in a harsh tone while narrowing my eyes at her.

"Can we talk?" She asks nervously, shifting the books that are in her hands.

"Why, so you can pretend to be my friend for a day and then completely embarrass me the next? Yeah, no thanks. Goodbye," I snap, the familiar feeling of betrayal bubbling in my chest. Hurt and regret flash through her blue eyes. Pulling my arm out of her hold, I walk to the cafeteria, passing lingering teenagers that witnessed our confrontation.

I sit down in my usual seat and groan when I realize I have work tonight. I work at the local cafe. I don't like it that much, but it's the only job I can work right now. I work Tuesdays, Thursdays and Saturdays from five to nine.

Today I decided that it would be best if I left my laptop in my locker so it doesn't get ruined. I get up from my seat and walk toward the lunch bar. Pulling a mere two dollars out of my pocket, I release a groan. I have enough money to get a bowl of fruit. I guess I'm being healthy today.

I get the fruit and pay the lunch lady. I walk back to my seat and plop down, angrily. This pisses me off. How am I supposed to take care of my son if I have no fucking money for myself? I need another job, or a better paying one.

I open the container of pineapple and strawberries and stab them angrily. I see Ezra wave and smile at me from his table. That brings a tiny smile to my face.

When lunch ends, I grab my things and start walking to my next class, which is Science. Science is personally one of my favorite subjects and It's surprisingly easy for me.

I take a seat and roll my eyes when I remember Emily is also in this class. *Fan-fucking-tastic.*

Can I ever catch a break?

Chapter Eight

ATHENA LEWIS

NO. I REALLY CAN'T catch a break, not even a small one. After Science class, the she-devil was waiting outside of the doorway with a mischievous smirk on her face.

So, I ignore her and start to walk past her. She takes this as an opportunity to stick her foot out, tripping me.

I stumble and try to catch myself, but that doesn't happen. I fall on my ass and all of my things fall on the floor, pens rolling away from me and papers scattered on the tiled floor. *Don't punch her. Don't punch her. You can't risk it.* I remind myself internally.

Everyone around me starts laughing and taking pictures. Tears fill my vision out of frustration and embarrassment. I sit there in humiliation, my breathing accelerating.

When I glance up, I see Emily in the crowd of students, glaring at Stacy, who shrugs and smirks. I close my eyes and focus on my breathing, trying not to have a panic attack in front of everyone. That would make everything worse.

I feel two strong arms pick me up and I snuggle into them, feeling some form of comfort. I already know who it is based on the minty smell, Ezra Kingston.

I open my eyes and see Stacy staring at us with her mouth dropped in disbelief. She straightens her posture and sends a flirty smile towards Ezra, who completely ignores it, instead he's staring at me and checking for injuries.

"What the hell are you all looking at? Get on with your lives! Go on, shoo!" Ezra shouts and the crowd of people soon filters out of the hallway and out of the building.

When everyone's gone, I push myself away from Ezra and wipe my tears. I start picking up my things that are spread out across the floor with Ezra's help.

I silently thank him for helping me and comforting me. I would have had a panic attack in front of everyone if he didn't help me.

"Are you alright?" Ezra asks me as we stand up off of the floor.

"I will be," I reply and give him a tiny smile.

"Why does she treat you like that?" He asks me while scratching the back of his head.

"If I'm being honest, I have a few hypotheses. Thank you though," I shrug while staring at him. "Bye," I add and start walking away.

"You're welcome. Bye Sunshine!" He shouts down the hallway. I roll my eyes, but the tiny smile doesn't leave my face, instead, it widens.

I walk to my locker and get my laptop. Walking through the school, I open the front office doors and sign myself out before starting to walk home.

I just want to go home cry and sleep, but I can't because I have to get ready for work. I can't miss it. I need as much money as I can get.

As I'm walking home it starts raining and someone drives right into a puddle, making it splash all over me. My eyes fill up with tears of frustration yet again.

And what makes it worse is that, that someone who is driving is Stacy fucking Harp. I clench my hands at my sides, forming tight fists.

"Stupid bitch!" She shouts at me as she speeds down the wet road.

"Are you fucking kidding me?" I shout at the cloudy sky as tears fall down my face.

When I get home, I'm practically sobbing out of frustration. My mom comes towards the living room when she hears the front door slam.

"Sweetie, what's wrong? What happened?" She asks with concern, seeing me covered in dirty water.

"I hate it here," I sob and she rushes over to me to hug me. She rubs my back, making me cry harder. It reminds me of when I lost Zeke.

I miss him so much. I miss Emily, I miss my dad, and I miss my son. *Why did everything have to go to shit?*

"Go take a shower and I'll make you some coffee and a sandwich," she tells me and then asks "Do you work today?" I nod and she nods back.

She rushes to the kitchen to make me something to eat. I love her so much. I don't know what I would do without her.

I make my way upstairs and strip out of my soaking wet clothes. Turning the shower on, I step in and almost moan at how good it feels to be out of the irritating and wet clothes.

I continue my shower and my thoughts end up going back to Ezra Kingston. Everything about him is fascinating to me. I have no idea how or why.

Chapter Nine

ATHENA LEWIS

I SLOWLY WALK DOWN the stairs after my warm and refreshing shower, already dressed in my work uniform. The uniform is pretty simple. It's a grey shirt with the cafe logo and name in black, blue jeans, black flats, and a cloth apron.

I walk into the kitchen with a frustrated sigh, but smile when I see my mom singing along to the music she's playing. It's wonderful to see her happy.

She looks at me and smiles. She walks over to me and takes my hands in hers and we start dancing along to the song with each other. We laugh with each other and catch our breath when the song ends.

I miss times like these.

"Here you go," she says and gives me my coffee and sandwich.

"Thank you," I thank her and then start eating.

"You're welcome," she replies. "When are you going to see Ian?" She takes a sip of her own coffee.

I finish chewing and then take a sip of coffee. "I'm going to try and see him later this week. It's Tuesday today so I'm going to try and see him Sunday," I reply and she nods slowly.

My phone buzzes with a notification and I pick it up.

Hey, Sunshine. What days are we working on the project? It reads and I think before typing back.

Um, how about Mondays and Wednesdays? I send.

Sounds great! He replies.

Okay, bye. I turn off my phone with a smile on my face.

My mom, meanwhile, is staring at me with a soft smile. "I haven't seen you smile like that since Zeke passed away."

"So who was it?" She asks, changing the subject when I look at the wooden table, instead of answering her question.

"Um, just a boy from my school I have an assignment with," I respond, shrugging. She smirks and tries to hide it by drinking more of her coffee.

"I talked to your therapist. You have an appointment scheduled for Sunday at noon," she informs me.

That works. I'll visit Ian after.

"Okay, thank you."

I check the time and it reads 4:28 pm. *Oh shit, I have to go.*

"Bye, mom. I love you," I tell her, kissing her cheek. I grab the things I need and run out of the house. I usually leave early since it takes a little while to get there.

I make it to the local cafe, Gina's, with five minutes to spare. I walk towards the back and nod at the other employees. I check-in and grab a notepad and pen.

I make my way towards a table and click my pen, getting ready to write down the orders. "Hi, welcome to Gina's. What can I get you?"

When I glance up, my eyes widen. Sitting there is Emily and her parents. Emily smiles at me, but her parents look at me with hatred.

"I'll have tea and the chicken noodle soup," Emily and Zeke's mom, Linda, tells me. I write it down with my hands shaking slightly.

The rest order what they want and I give the order to the cook and take a deep breath. I take a couple of orders from different tables and then pick up the Colt's food. Walking back to their table, I set it down.

"Enjoy," I say with a fake smile on my face.

I walk towards the staff only room and take a couple of breaths to calm my nerves. Then I walk back towards the main area.

"There is a hair in our food!" A voice shouts from the front of the cafe.

I walk faster and see Linda complaining about her food to Gina, the owner of the small and local cafe.

"That little bitch probably did it," she snarls at me.

"What? No, I did not," I argue back.

"What would you like me to do about it?" Gina asks them, making Linda smirk.

"Fire her," she says. My mouth falls open and I look at Gina, begging her not to.

"Athena," she starts, rolling her eyes as Linda starts to complain even more.

"Wait!" Emily speaks up. "Athena didn't. My mom pulled a piece of her hair out and put it in her food. I saw her do it," She rushes out and I look at her in shock.

Why would she stand up for me? She said and I quote, *"I hate you! I want nothing to do with you! You're nothing but a sad bitch who will never be successful!"*

Linda and her husband pale and Gina looks at them, now pissed off. "Get out of here before I call the cops," she threatens and they quickly leave. Emily smiles at me and follows them out.

I look at Gina and she gives me a sympathetic smile. She knows about Ian and Zeke. I know she wouldn't fire me. She gives me a hug and then we go back to work.

"Here is your paycheck," Gina says, giving me my check. I thank her and then open it.

It reads $246. "Why did you raise it $26?" I ask her with tears in my eyes.

She smiles at me. "I've noticed you've been struggling so I decided to raise it."

I hug her. "Thank you so much," I wipe my tears away.

"Don't thank me, you deserved it."

After work, I walk back home and then shower and go to bed, readying myself for even more nightmares.

Chapter Ten

EZRA KINGSTON

I SIT AT MY WHITE desk and stare out the window. It started raining a little while ago, so now I watch as tiny drops of rain slide down the glass. My thoughts soon drift to the raven-haired girl with the name of Athena Lewis.

I've noticed her at school before. *How could I not she's fucking beautiful?* Athena used to be a very open and outgoing person, but that all changed when her boyfriend Zeke died in a car crash.

Ever since then, she has been very closed off and quiet.

She always seems stressed. When I saw her on the ground with a look of fear in her eyes, I knew I had to help her. Nobody deserves to be treated like that.

I messaged her earlier about the essay arrangements and I also wanted to see how she was doing.

"Ezra get your ass down here!" I'm startled from my thoughts by my drunk father yelling for me.

I quickly run down the stairs and walk into the living room. "Yes?" I ask, wanting to be nowhere near him.

"Go get me more beer," he groans and hands me $24. "Don't come back until you get fifteen cans," he adds and then lays on the couch, turning on the TV.

"Oh, and when is your bitch of a mother coming home?" He asks me before I walk out the door. I clench my hands into fists.

"I don't know. She's not a bitch, you are." I reply, turning to look at him. I shake my head when loud snores escape his mouth and then walk out the door.

My mother is definitely not a bitch. She is kind, loving and hard-working. She has a kind heart which is one of the main reasons why she stays with my asshole of a father.

I walk in the pouring rain towards the store. It's pretty dark and still raining by the time I get there. I open the door of the gas station and nod at the cashier.

I grab the cans of beer and give the guy, whose name tag reads Toby, the money. He puts the cans in the bags and hands them to me. "Would you like your receipt?" He asks in a bored tone.

"No, but thank you," I reply and he nods. I pick the bags up and leave the store.

I start walking home in the pouring rain. Many cars pass me and I see someone walk out of Gina's cafe and then walk in the glow of a streetlight with a tiny smile on her face.

I make it back home and give my father his beer. Then I go to my bathroom to take a shower with one question in my mind.

What's your secret Athena?

Chapter Eleven

ATHENA LEWIS

IT'S WEDNESDAY TODAY AND that means Ezra is coming over to my house to work on the essay. My mom said it was okay for him to come over and she said she would buy snacks for us.

I'm in History at the moment and Ezra and I are working on the essay. I look over at him and see him staring at me.

I raise an eyebrow. "What?"

"Nothing" he shrugs. "But wipe that frown off of your face. It will give you wrinkles like an old lady," he leans back in his chair.

I stare at him and then slowly smile, picturing me as an old lady.
Ezra looks at me weirdly.

"That smile is creeping me out," he says, cautiously, with wide eyes.

"Oh, well," I narrow my eyes at him. He shakes his head and turns back to his laptop.

"Athena is something bothering you?" Mr. Wilson asks me from his wooden desk that sits at the front of the room.

Yes, your voice. I think to myself and laugh quietly.

"Nope," I respond and then look at my laptop to read through more articles.

I quickly clean the living room and place the snacks on the coffee table. Ezra is supposed to be coming over in about fifteen minutes and I'm slightly nervous.

Nobody has come over in years, especially someone new. Emily, Zeke, and I used to hang out alot and then the car crash happened. I still remember being so excited to tell Zeke I was pregnant.

We planned everything as soon as I told him. We were going out for dinner, but then it started snowing and then... I'm interrupted by a knock on the door. I walk over to it and wipe my sweaty palms on my leggings. Reaching for the doorknob, I turn the handle and open the door.

"Hello, Sunshine," Ezra says with his laptop in his hands and a smile on his face. Does he ever frown?

"Hi, Ezra," I reply with a half-smile on my face.

I move over and invite him in the house. He walks in and glances around. "Your house is very cozy," he compliments. "Where are your parents?"

"My mom is at work," I reply.

"What about your dad?" He asks and I stay silent.

"Okay, let's get started on the essay," he smiles, changing the subject when I don't answer his question. I nod and we awkwardly sit on the couch.

Eventually, we get comfortable and get straight to work. We read several articles and then add some of the facts that explain interesting things about pollution onto the google doc.

★★★

"Let's play twenty questions," Ezra says suddenly, making my hands pause over the keyboard. Turning to him, I nod slowly and he smirks.

"What's something you're afraid of?" He asks and I look at him skeptically.

"Cars," I reply simply. He nods and realization soon washes over his features.

"Why do you call me Sunshine?"

"Well, I wasn't sure of calling you it at first. When I called you it randomly, you started smiling more, so I declared it as your nickname."

"Why does Emily treat you like shit?"

"She blames me for Zeke's death along with her parents."

"It wasn't your fault though," he frowns.

"What's your favorite color?" I ask and stare into his eyes.

"Green."

"Do you trust me?" He asks and I slowly nod. I do trust him.

That's where our game of twenty questions ends, even though it was a couple of questions.

Soon enough Ezra says he has to go home and I walk him to the door. Turning around, he stares into my eyes, smiling and slowly wraps his arms around me, pulling me into a comforting hug. I wrap my arms around him, the feeling of something warm and calm forming in my stomach.

"Goodnight, Sunshine," he whispers in my ear and then all too soon, he pulls away from the hug.

"Goodnight, Ezra."

I turn to go back inside. "Oh, and Sunshine?" He asks and I turn around and look at him.

"Yes?"

"You should really smile more," he winks before walking away. I smile and walk back inside, my stomach feeling like a gooey mess.

Chapter Twelve

ATHENA LEWIS

Walking into the brick building, I make my way over to the reception desk to check in.

"Name?" the receptionist asks with a friendly smile, chewing on a piece of bubble gum, her hands positioned over the black keyboard. Her brown eyes look at me in question and a few strands of her brown hair, that's in a bun, fall on her face.

"Sorry. Athena Lewis," I clear my throat, the feeling of being alone creeping its way into my head.

"Don't worry about it," she smiles, her manicured fingers rapidly typing against the keyboard. "You're all checked in and Dr. Barnes should be out shortly."

When I'm checked in, I take a seat in the plastic chairs and think about Ian while I wait for my therapist to call me back to her office. After therapy, I can go and see him.

"Athena Lewis." My head shoots up when my name is called. I get up and walk over to my therapist, Dr. Barnes. She smiles at me and leads me to her office. Dr. Barnes is a pretty and nice lady, a smile is always placed on her painted lips wherever we have appointments. Her office smells of disinfectant wipes most of the time too. Weird, I know.

She sits in her chair and I sit on the leather couch that's across from her, folding my hands in my lap.

"So, how have you been, Athena?" she asks and I stay silent for a little while, listening to the ticking of the clock that hangs above her office door on the wall.

I look up at her and frown. "Not great. The nightmares are back and I'm just very stressed. I have been working my ass off, and I want to see my son because I miss him." She nods and writes what I said on her notepad.

"How are things with your son? He's seven months now, correct?"

"Correct and I visited him over the winter break as much as I could," I tell her.

"Okay, and how is school going for you?"

"Um, not well. Stacy tripped me the other day and I almost had a panic attack in front of most of the twelfth grade. But my essay partner calmed me down."

"So this essay partner, do you trust him or her?"

"Ezra," I say and she looks at me confused. "His name is Ezra and yes I do."

"Does he make you happy?"

Yes, he does, so much that it scares me.

"Very."

"That's great. I'm happy for you, Athena," she smiles at me.

"Thank you," I thank her and shift to a more comfortable sitting position.

"So, back to your nightmares, has anything changed when you have them?" She asks and looks up at me after she writes on her notepad.

"Yes, I had one where I lost Ian in the car crash. I couldn't find him and everything turned black. Then just like that, everything vanished and I woke up. I felt so helpless. That nightmare scared the shit out of me," I tell with unshed tears in my eyes. She gives me a box of tissues and I wipe the tears away.

After my therapy session, I walk down the busy road, towards my neighborhood. The town I live in, in Seattle is pretty small and everything is within a walkable distance.

The town has a pretty small population and a wonderful low crime rate. It's sunny sometimes, but other times it's like Forks from Twilight, rainy and cold.

Ian thankfully lives with his temporary adoptive family within a walkable distance. His adoptive family is my mom and I's family friends, Annalise and Lee Monroe. They aren't able to have kids of their own and I got pregnant while they were looking to adopt. I gave them the legal rights and custody of Ian until the end of the school year.

I make it to the front door of Lee and Annalise's beautiful house. It's my dream house. It has a white picket fence, flowers in the flowerbed, and a pool in the backyard along with a swing set. It's the perfect home for Ian, but he belongs with me. I'm his mother.

I take a deep breath and knock on the door. Soon the door opens and I come face to face with Annalise, who has Ian in her arms. She welcomes me in with a warm smile. Annalise and Lee are from China and came to the USA for a better life for their older parents and family. Annalise has brown narrowed eyes and mid length brown hair, while Lee has brown narrowed eyes, and a buzz cut with a beard.

"Hey, come in," she invites me in and closes the door behind me. I take Ian from her and look into his familiar blue eyes, eyes he inherited from me and brown hair he inherited from Zeke.

"Hi, Anna," I smile at her and then nod at Lee, acknowledging him.

"Mama," he giggles and snuggles into me. My eyes tear up and I hold him closer to me. I missed having him in my arms.

Chapter Thirteen

ATHENA LEWIS

MY EYES WATER WHEN Ian walks towards me, wobbling with every small step he takes. Annalise said he started walking a little while ago. She said she didn't get it on video, so I missed his first steps. Guilt bubbles in my stomach. *How could I miss something so important?*

I wipe my tears away and kiss his forehead, making him giggle and smile at me. I brush some hair out of his eyes, looking at his bright smile. He's my happy little boy.

Lee and Annalise watch us with smiles on their faces. "Athena even though you don't think you are, you're an amazing mother," Annalise says and Lee nods, agreeing with her.

"I'm so thankful for you guys. If I didn't have you I don't think I would be making it through school. I love you guys for everything you've done for me and Ian."

They walk over to me and pull me into a hug while I hold Ian in my arms. He looks around confused and I smile at him.

"We will take care of Ian until you graduate or however long you need," Annalise tells me. "He's an angel."

"Thank you," I pull away from the hug and sit on the ground.

Ian walks to me and then back to Annalise and Lee for a while. I smile every time he makes it to me. "Good job!" I coo and kiss his chubby cheeks, making him giggle with a happy smile.

"Mama, I go," Ian begs when I make it to the door, getting ready to leave. I look at him sadly as he pouts with unshed tears in his eyes.

"Not today buddy, but soon I promise," I kiss his head. I look into his watery blue eyes and turn around to leave.

"Mama!" Ian screams, but I close the door and start walking home with guilt and watery eyes of my own.

I find a bench in the local park. The sun just started going down and I watch some families start to leave, listening to the birds chirp for a while.

I look down to my right, staring at the bench. Zeke and I used to come here. This was our spot.

"May I sit here?" Someone asks. I look up at the familiar green eyes and nod. Ezra sits down and stays quiet.

"Why are you crying?" He asks after a long period of silence.

"I'm just going through some things right now," I reply and wipe my face with my sleeve.

"Aren't we all?" He mumbles. I look at him and he shrugs. "You can tell me anything. You can trust me."

I know I can.

"I know, and the same goes for you," I whisper and watch the sunlight slowly disappear.

"It was nice seeing you again, Sunshine. I'll see you tomorrow," Ezra says and then gets up.

"It was nice seeing you too, Ezra," I whisper and get up also. Ezra and I go our separate ways. I take one more look at the bench and then leave the dark park.

I slowly walk home, enjoying the quiet and fresh cool air. Late night walks are the best thing. They give me a lot of time to think and pass time.

Soon, I make it home and walk upstairs. I tell my mom goodnight and go to my room for a shower.

After my shower, I sit at my desk and log into my laptop, so I can start writing the next chapter of my book. I groan when it starts making weird noises. Stacy pretty much broke my laptop with her stunt to gain more popularity. *Wonderful.*

That bitch.

I don't have money to fix it, absolutely none. I'm saving all I have for an apartment and essential things for myself and Ian.

I angrily close my laptop and crawl into bed. I want to hit that bitch so much, but I can't. If I do I might not be able to get custody of Ian and I'll be deemed as a violent mother or something outrageous like that.

It takes me a little while to fall asleep, but I eventually do and find myself in the familiar black nothingness, until it forms into the familiar and haunting scenery.

Chapter Fourteen

ATHENA LEWIS

THE NEXT MORNING I GET out of bed a lot happier. Yesterday's therapy session helped me a lot. It felt amazing to talk to someone else about my nightmares. I really can't talk to my mom about them because she's always at work.

I still tell her bits and pieces and that I have them. She tries her best to help me by comforting me. She does as much as she can and for that I'm thankful.

Ezra didn't show up to school at all today. I was kind of disappointed, but I ignored it. He probably slept in, but I couldn't help the nagging feeling I had.

Emily said "Hi," to me today and it confused me. I don't know why she is trying to talk to me. She said she hated me months ago, and much more than that. I do miss her. I miss my best friend, my sister from another mister.

Stacy didn't do anything, but call me names in the hallway today. I can handle name-calling, but physical touching is a no-no.

There is also a new girl who transferred here from Dresden, Germany. Her name is June. She is pretty nice, and we have a few classes together.

She's like a very bubbly and happy person. If you think about it, she's almost like a female Ezra.

We exchanged phone numbers after she told Stacy to fuck off. She asked me for mine and told me I can come to her whenever I need to talk.

I have been sitting on the couch for an hour, staring at my phone. Ezra was supposed to be here an hour ago. I texted him an hour ago, but he never replied.

I'm starting to get really worried. *What if he's dead? Okay, I'm overthinking now.* I'm startled out of my thoughts as someone pounds on my door. I slowly get up to open the door.

Ezra stumbles into my house with a black eye and a bloody nose. *Did he get into a fight? Whose cereal did he piss in?* I immediately make him sit on the couch and quickly grab some ice and a clean, wet cloth.

He groans when I place the ice on his bruised eye. "Sorry," I mumble.

"It's okay."

After I wipe his bloody nose, I sigh and look at him expectantly. I'm waiting for him to explain why he is bruised and bloody, sitting on my couch.

"I was jumped on my way here," he grunts, shifting on the couch, making me roll my eyes. He's lying. Ezra could definitely win a fight. He has the muscles and the build.

"Mhm," I mutter. *Then how come he doesn't have his laptop with him?* "I'm not going to make you tell me," I reply after a little while. He closes his eyes and winces in pain. Feeling bad, I drop the questions that are swimming in my head.

"You can sleep here. If you want," I tell him, making him nod. My mom wouldn't mind. She's already asleep anyway and it's not like we're dating or going to screw.

"Thank you."

"Yeah."

I walk downstairs after I grab Ezra a blanket and pillow. Our fingers brush when I give them to him, warm tingles shooting up my arm. Brushing it off as just the static from the fuzzy blanket, I help make his bed on the couch and Ezra groans in pain when he shifts on his right side.

"Never better," he smiles, masking the pain he's in. I nod and go to the kitchen to grab him a glass of water and ibuprofen.

Walking back to the living room from the kitchen, I give him the water and ibuprofen, watching as he gratefully swallows the two pills with a gulp of ice water.

"Thanks."

"Don't mention it," I mutter and walk towards the light switch. "Goodnight, Ezra," I whisper.

"Night, Sunshine," he closes his eyes and I smile before turning off the lights.

I crawl into bed and think about the way that could have led Ezra to being beat up. *Is he in a gang? Is he being abused?* That wouldn't make sense, he's always happy.

Well, some people hide behind masks or they see the positive things no matter how bad their life is. *What is he hiding?* I want to know and I want to be there for him, as a friend.

What's your secret Ezra?

Chapter Fifteen

EZRA KINGSTON

HOW AM I SUPPOSED TO tell Athena that my father beat me up because I refused to buy him even more cans of beer? I don't want him to drink anymore, so I told him no. Maybe I should have kept my mouth shut.

I had nowhere else to go. All of my friends are fake, and Athena feels like the only person I can trust, besides my mom of course.

I'm glad she let me stay the night. I couldn't go back home and risk getting my ass beat again. I would never hit him back. He's my father and he's in a tough spot. He lost his job and then his mother passed away.

I know Athena doesn't believe that I was jumped, but I'm glad she didn't question me further. I don't want anyone to know what goes on in my house. It's better that way.

I am now laying in the dark on Athena's couch. I grit my teeth in pain while I try to get comfortable. My right side is bruised from my father kicking me. I lay down and close my eyes, focusing on my thoughts.

My mom is still at work. She's a doctor and she works night shifts. We have a lot more than an average amount of money thanks to her and her hard work.

I take another sip of the water that Athena gave me before she went upstairs. It helps my headache a little bit. Laying my head down again on the couch, I close my eyes and listen to the ticking of the clock she has on her wall. Her house is really cozy and warm looking if that makes sense.

Humming softly, I slowly fall asleep.

I wake up to the sound of someone making a ton of noise, followed by a loud bang and a faint, "Dammit!"

Athena walks into the living room and closes her eyes, leaning against the wall. Powder is on her clothing and her hair is in a messy bun, a few strands of her black hair falling into her face. She groans and opens her eyes. Her eyes grow wide with embarrassment and her cheeks heat up when she sees me looking at her with an amused eyebrow raised.

"Morning, Sunshine," I greet and shift on the couch, hiding my pain with a smile.

"Don't even start," she groans. I look at the clock on the wall to check the time. It's 5:36 am and it's Tuesday.

I slowly get off of the couch when I start to smell something burning. Walking towards her, I point at the kitchen entrance. "Something's burning," I tell her. She rubs her temples and groans even louder.

She smiles at me innocently. "That would be the pancakes," she hurries into the kitchen and I follow after her.

I laugh, making my body ache when I see her rushing around the kitchen. There is pancake mix on the floor and eggs cracked open on the counter. The kitchen is an absolute mess.

"I'm never going to try and make breakfast again," Athena crosses her arms over her chest as she looks over the mess.

I clear my throat and she looks at me. "Let me cook."

"You're injured," she deadpans, slipping on egg yolk and almost falling on top of me. "Sorry," her face turns a shade of red with embarrassment

"I'll be fine and it's the least I can do," I reply.

"Fine, go for it," she shrugs and sits down at the table to watch me.

I immediately start making food and clean up the mess along the way. *Gordon Ramsay, who?*

Chapter Sixteen

ATHENA LEWIS

"VOILA," EZRA SMILES PROUDLY as he sets a plate of mouth-watering food in front of me. The plate consists of bacon, eggs, and pancakes. My stomach aches, begging me to eat the warm food. Slowly, I start eating when Ezra takes a seat next to me.

My mom comes downstairs a little while after we finish eating. "Oh, hello," she greets and gets some food for herself before sitting down across from us. "Athena, you should have told me someone was coming over," she scolds and I look at her sheepishly.

"Um, mom, this is Ezra," I tell her after clearing my throat. She looks at me with wide eyes and mouths, 'Ezra, Ezra?'

She turns to Ezra. "It's nice to finally meet you, Ezra," she says to him in a motherly voice, shaking his hand. Subconsciously, I glare at her hand that's in his.

He smiles at her. "It's nice to meet you too, Ms. Lewis."

"Just call me Rhea, dear," she laughs, waving him off. "He's charming and respectful," she smirks at me before getting up from the table.

That he his.

I blush from my seat, making Ezra chuckle.

God, help me. His laugh could make anyone turn to goo.

"You're welcome here anytime, Ezra."

That went well.

Ezra and I walk into school together, getting a few surprised and bored looks from people. I spot Stacy leaning against a locker with Emily. When she notices us, she smirks and walks over to us.

"Well let me guess, you're sleeping with the football player. Finally over the dead boyfriend?" She asks in fake pity, laughing like a witch. My eyes fill up with tears and I see Emily's fill up with tears from her spot next to Stacy.

Nobody talks about Zeke like that. Nobody!

Consumed with a massive amount of anger, I pull my fist back and punch her in the face. She falls to the ground and I get on top of her, screaming as I continue punching her.

"Athena!" Ezra shouts from behind me, but I ignore him.

"Never mention him again!" My scream echoes through the crowded hallway as strong arms wrap around me and lift me off of her "Bitch!"

"Ms. Lewis, fighting is unacceptable here," the principal, Mr. Baxter, scolds me.

"She deserved it," I grumble. Meanwhile, Stacy is crying in the chair next to me, acting like the fake bitch she is. I smirk discreetly as I look at the black eye I left her. *She had it coming.*

"How so?" He asks, folding his hands on his desk.

"She has poured hot chili on me, dumped her food on my laptop and I, and she has been calling me names non stop," I list off, using my fingers for effect. "She had it coming," I repeat and he nods and looks at Stacy, who is wiping her wet eyes, sniffling.

"She's lying!" She shouts, turning to me to send me a glare.

"No, she is not. I've watched the tapes from the cameras. You're a bully and we do not like bullying here," he tells her, now looking at her. Stacy pales and I smirk slightly.

"Why didn't you do anything about it if you knew?" I ask, glaring at him.

"Well, uh."

"You know what? Nevermind," I wave him off, slumping back in the surprisingly comfortable office chair.

"Stacy, you are suspended for two weeks," he then looks at me. "Athena, you have detention after school today," he tells us and I nod, deciding not to argue. Stacy begins arguing with him and I leave the office with an eye roll.

Thank God detention is two hours long. I won't miss work. School ends at two and If I rush home, I can make it to work.

★★★

When I leave the office, I spot June and Ezra leaning against the lockers, next to the office door. *Why are they here again?*

"Oh thank the heavens you're alright," June says, her german accent rolling off of her tongue. She wraps her arms around me and I smile before hugging her back.

"So what happened? Are you expelled?" Ezra fires off questions and I smile at him, grateful that he cares.

"Would you care if I was?" I ask, watching as his cheeks start to turn pink.

"Well, yeah," he mumbles, rubbing the back of his neck, his shirt riding up and exposing some of his sculpted chest. *Sweet Jesus.*

"So are you?" June asks, making me turn my attention to her, instead of Ezra's Greek god-like features.

"No, but, I have detention after school today," I tell them as we walk to English.

"Did Stacy get in trouble?" Ezra shifts the books in his hand, looking at me as we walk down the hallway. *Yes, finally.*

"She's suspended for two weeks."

"Two weeks, that's all?" He frowns, his eyebrows pulling together.

"I've only been here a few days and she's done damage to you than my homophobic parents," June shakes her head, frowning and mumbling under her breath.

"At least it's something," I shrug.

"Well, Mr. Baxter needs to do more than sit on his ass and bang Mrs. Kay," Ezra grumbles. I stifle a laugh. There's this rumor that has been going around the school for years. Everyone thinks Mr. Baxter and the Special Ed teacher, Mrs. Kay, are screwing. I wouldn't be surprised if they were.

When we get to English, June sits with her *partner*, Summer. June told me the other day that she is a lesbian. She was scared that I wouldn't be friends with her if she was. I told her she has nothing to worry about and that I fully support the LGBTQ community. I don't understand how some parents don't support their kids. *They're your flesh and blood, get over yourself.*

Taking a seat next to Ezra, we start working on the essay. Yet again, I read through articles and take notes. Ezra, of course, does the same.

Now at the end of the day, I walk to the detention room. I open the door and walk-in, giving the detention teacher my slip and then I take a seat. Taking a seat near the window, I begin thinking about Ezra.

Chapter Seventeen

EZRA KINGSTON

Slowly, I walk into my house and close the white door behind me. I sigh in relief when I see my father passed out on the couch, yet again.

My mom walks into the living room, looking tired with tears rolling down her cheeks and I frown. She shouldn't feel like this. The best decision she could make is throwing my dad out.

She starts picking up the empty beer bottles, but I quickly grab them from her and give her a stern look.

I will do it.

"Mom, I got this. Go take a nap. You have work, and you're tired," I tell her. She rubs her eyes and then nods.

"Thank you, hun," she kisses me on my forehead and walks upstairs, the wooden steps creaking with every step she takes.

"Asshole," I whisper and glare at the sleeping man on *my* couch.

Picking up the trash and beer bottles with my fist clenched, I try my hardest not to pull my father off of the couch and kick him out. He is an asshole, an asshole that needs to get his shit together.

I walk into the football locker room and change into my football gear. I have football practice on Tuesdays and Thursdays and on days that I don't have practice, I catch up on school work.

I jog out to the field and wave at some of the other guys on the team. We all stand in a circle and wait for our coach, Coach Perry, to tell us what to do. Coach Perry is a pretty nice guy. He is in his mid thirties and has a trimmed beard and a muscular build, light brown skin, a bald head and brown eyes.

"Okay, everyone, run back and forth seven times and then do five stretches," he instructs. Everyone nods, ready to start practice.

"Yes, coach," everyone on the team says, making him smile triumphantly.

"Ezra, come here. The rest of you, begin!"

My feet move on the grass as I jog over to Coach Perry. "Yes, coach?"

"How is everything at home?" He asks, his hands on his hips as he looks at me in questions.

I clear my throat. "Things are rough… but they are better than before." Coach Perry is the only one that knows about the situation in my house. I made him promise not to tell anyone, and so far, he's kept it.

"Is he still drinking?"

"Always."

He shakes his head. "I'm always here if you need to talk, and so is the rest of the team," he pats my shoulder before nodding at the field. "Go catch up."

Jogging away from him, I run up and down the field a total of fourteen times. Moving to the stretches, I find an open spot on the field and start to stretch. I'm a little ahead of everyone because I'm not flirting with girls. I'm not interested in those particular girls.

I'm onl-

"Get into your teams!" Coach Perry shouts, blowing his whistle. I run over towards my group and wait for further instructions.

We get into position and Coach Perry blows his whistle. One person hikes the ball and then I start running down the field. Out of the corner of my eye, I see Athena wave at me from her spot on the bleachers. Getting distracted by her, I get tackled by John, a player on the other team.

"Sorry!" Athena shouts, waving frantically with a guilty look.

"It's alright, Sunshine!" I shout back and she rolls her eyes with a smile on her face. I push John off of me and get up.

"Bye, Ezra!" She starts walking away and I watch her retreating figure.

"She's hot, what's her name?" John asks me with a smirk on his face, his brown eyes locked on her ass. *Fucking perv.* I scrunch my face up.

I glare at him. "Fuck off. She's not interested in your player ass," I sneer, jealousy surging throughout my body and he chuckles in response.

"Oh, so you have eyes for her, is that it, Kingston?" He smirks, looking at the place Athena was just at.

"Maybe, maybe not. It's not your business anyway," I reply with clenched hands. "Don't go anywhere near her."

"Don't worry," he jabs his finger into my chest. "According to Stacy, she's a skank anyway."

"Touch me one more time and I'll break your fucking nose," I push his hand away with a glare. I walk away from him and back to my group, who are watching us curiously, probably anticipating a fight.

My eyes glance down at my clenched hands. *Why do I feel this way? What is it?* I've never felt this way about someone and It's freaking me out.

After football practice, I decided to stop by at Gina's café for dinner since it's around six pm.

I get in my car and drive on the familiar road. Reaching for the dial, I turn on the radio and plug the aux cord into my phone, putting on *Last Time I Say Sorry* by *John Legend and Kane Brown*.

The music flows through the speaker and I take a right, turning onto another road. The sun is slowly starting to set and the streetlights are just now turning on.

"I won't say I'm sorry over and over," I tap my fingers against the steering wheel.

I pull into the small parking lot of the café and park. Taking the keys out of the ignition, I open my door and get out, locking my car behind me.

"Welcome to Gina's café, what can I get you?" A familiar voice asks and I look up and smile at her. She smiles back, putting a strand of her black hair behind her ear

She truly is beautiful.

"Hi, Sunshine," I place my menu down. I grin and her cheeks turn a light shade of pink.

"Hi, Ezra, what would you like?" She asks again, pressing the pen's tip against the notepad as she waits for my order.

"I would like a burger and fries with a Dr. Pepper," I tell her and she nods while writing it down on her notepad.

"Okay, that will be out soon."

"Thank you," I give her my menu. Our fingers brush against each others, creating an unknown feeling in my stomach. The only way I can describe it is, warm and comforting.

Why does my heart speed up whenever I'm around her? Why do I feel nervous when she talks to me? What is this? Am I dying? I can't die before I get a chance with her.

Chapter Eighteen

EZRA KINGSTON

"HERE YOU GO," ATHENA says as she places my food in front of me, my mouth slightly watering at the smell and sight of it.

"Thank you," I smile and she nods and smiles a small smile, but at least it's something.

"Tell me if I can get you anything else."

"I will," I smile back at her. With a smile, she walks away to take more orders. Surprisingly, I'm not the only one here. The café is rarely busy.

After I finish my food, I pay and leave Athena a twenty-five dollar tip on the table. Walking out of the café and across the parking lot to my car, I unlock it and pull the door open. Climbing in, I close the door behind me and stick the key in the ignition.

I sit in the car and watch from my window as Athena picks up my tip. She smiles and I smile myself, glad that I made her happy. I also left her a note on a napkin under the tip saying, *Bye Sunshine*.

I turn on the radio and put the car in drive. Pulling out of my parking spot and the parking lot, I drive home with a smile on my face. But that smile turns into a worried frown when I walk through the front door of my house.

Picture frames are smashed along with several beer bottles on the ground. Arguing echoes through the house from upstairs.

I follow the sound to my parent's room. "I don't care! Get the fuck out of my house! I have had enough of you and your shit!"

I open their bedroom door and see my mom going through the closet and throwing my dad's clothes into a suitcase. My father, however, is sitting on the bed with his head in his hands.

"I'm not leaving!" He screams at her, standing up and walking over to her. *No you don't, you bastard.*

"Mom?" I ask, moving over to her, putting distance between my father and her. "What's going on?"

"Your father is leaving. I'm not dealing with him anymore. If he wants to sleep with other girls, he can do it in his own house, not in mine!" She shouts the last part at my dad.

"I don't love you anymore!" He shouts at her, taking the suitcase from her with tears in his eyes.

"Get out!" She screams, tears rapidly falling from her eyes. "And don't come back!"

He leaves the room and the front door slams, telling us that he left. *Hopefully for good this time.*

My mom sits on the edge of the bed and starts sobbing and I quickly rush over to comfort her.

"I love him so much," she sobs into my shirt. "I can't deal with him anymore though," she continues. "Enough is enough."

I rub her back as she sobs into my shoulder. "I know, mom. I'm sorry, but he is an asshole," I tell her. "You deserve so much more."

We both do.

She nods against my shoulder, but cries even harder than before. Eventually, she falls asleep from crying. She has work tonight, so I decide to let her sleep for a little while. I leave the room and close the door quietly behind me.

Walking down the wooden stairs and into the living room with a huff, I grab a garbage bag and start cleaning up the glass and smashed beer bottles. I get the vacuum cleaner and start vacuuming the small pieces of glass that I can't pick up with my hands.

After I do that, I clean up all the food wrappers and women's clothes that are on the couch. *Ew, she probably has an STD or something.* If she didn't before, she definitely has one now. Continuing to clean, I try to ignore the fact that he cheated on my mom, his wife.

Once I'm finished with the cleaning, I wash my hands and then make my mom some coffee. I pour the coffee into a thermal mug and put some creamer in it.

Eventually, she walks downstairs in her work clothes and grabs the coffee. "Thank you, hun," she sips the coffee.

"You're welcome, mom," I reply, smiling and giving her car keys to her.

She kisses my head and grabs her things. When she leaves for work, I'm left at home alone and bored. It's dark out, so I can't throw the football at the fence. Instead, I go upstairs and start doing some of my homework that's due on Friday.

I sit at my desk and start doing the math homework and I quickly finish it. I'm pretty good at math, but it's not my favorite. I'm just good with numbers I guess.

I check the clock and yawn when it says nine-thirty pm. I take a shower and then lay in bed, not being able to fall asleep. I roll over and grab my phone from my nightstand and before I know it I'm clicking on Athena's contact.

Chapter Nineteen

ATHENA LEWIS

As soon as I'm just about to fall asleep, my phone dings with a notification. Groaning, I stare at my wall. *Why does someone have to text me?* I want to sleep.

I sit up and turn on the lamp that's placed on my bedside table. Grabbing my phone, I unplug it from its charger. My mood changes when I see who dared to wake me up.

I open Ezra's message. *Hey, Sunshine, how are you? :)*

Hi, Ezra, I'm doing alright. I'm just tired. I type back, my phone screen blinding me slightly.

Did I wake you up? His next message reads.

I sigh. *Kind of, but it's alright. What are you up to?*

I'm just laying in bed and decided to text you because I can't sleep. I read his message with wide eyes. *I was thinking about you, too.*

My cheeks heat up a little bit when I read the last part. *He was thinking about me?*

Oh really? I bite my lip.

Yes, really. He sends back.

I laugh and take a deep breath. *Are we flirting?*

My phone vibrates with another message from him. *Get some sleep, Sunshine. I'll see you tomorrow, sorry for waking you. Goodnight.*

It's alright, you too. Goodnight. I send it and then turn off my phone.

I walk into English with a smile on my face. I'm happy about Ezra and I's friendship. I trust him, but I don't want him to run for the hills the first chance he gets when he finds out I have a child. I don't want to lose him as a friend. I haven't had someone like him in a while.

I sit down in my seat, next to Ezra. June and Summer walk into the classroom, holding hands, making my eyebrows raise. *They just met, didn't they?*

June laughs when she sees my confused face. "We were talking over the internet for a little while already, and now that I'm here in the flesh we are officially together," she explains with a big smile on her face.

"It's nice to formally meet you. I've seen you around school when stuff went down with the wicked witch of the West," Summer laughs. That's a new nickname for Stacy. Ezra laughs and I do too.

After we chat for a little more, they go sit down in their seats. I turn to my computer and do the usual work for the essay.

After school, I walk back home, following the familiar sidewalk. It's sunny today which is great and it fits my mood perfectly, happy.

My phone buzzes in my pocket and I stop walking. I grab my phone out and look at the message. The familiar frown finds itself back on my face.

Hey, Athena, Lee and I decided we are going to take Ian on a two week vacation, the message reads.

My heart sinks as I read the message. I won't be able to see my baby for two weeks.

Why did you guys decide to go on a trip? Especially now. My fingers fly across the keyboard.

Lee and I have been stressed so we decided we should take a vacation. She replies.

Okay, stay safe, and have fun! I type back, the words I type not meeting my mood. *Send me pictures of Ian too!*

I turn off my phone and continue walking home with a frown on my face. I swear I'm going to get wrinkles by the time I'm forty.

I understand that they have been working hard and are stressed, but I won't see my son for two weeks. I don't know if I can go so long without seeing his happy face.

I make it home with a deeper frown on my face and I sit on the couch. Taking my computer out of my bookbag, I start to write while I wait for Ezra to get here.

My hands pause over the keyboard as someone knocks on the door. I place my laptop on the table and walk to the door. My fingers grip the cold metal door knob and I open it, smiling at Ezra.

"Hi, Sunshine."

"Hi, Ezra."

I let him in and close the door behind us. Ezra follows me to the living room and we sit down on the couch. I sit crisscrossed and grab my laptop off of the table. Ezra and I begin working on the essay and I laugh at some of the jokes he tells me.

I turn my head and smile at him. Ezra and I stare at each other. His eyes flicker to my lips and mine do the same. I look into his glimmering green eyes and we both slowly start leaning in.

My heart beats rapidly in my chest, anticipating our lips to touch each others. I want nothing more than to kiss him, to feel his lips on mine. I haven't felt this way in a while.

Ezra and I's lips meet one another's. My eyes flutter closed and our lips move in sync. Ezra pulls me onto his lap and my hands go behind his neck, pulling him closer to me. His hands stay on my waist and our chests touch as we kiss. Bliss. That's the word to describe how kissing him feels.

I haven't felt this way in such a long time, too long of a time. Ezra kisses my lips lightly after he pulls away.

He looks at me with his eyes glistening brighter than ever. I smile at him and he smiles back. "I've been wanting to do that for a while, ever since I saw you around school," he whispers, his green eyes searching mine.

Glancing down at the position we are in, I blush and I climb off of his lap and sit next to him, trying to calm my erratic breathing.

"I haven't felt this way in a while," I whisper back to him. "But I like the way you make me feel."

"I like the way you make me feel too," he tells me, his smile growing.

He's changing me, and I don't mind one bit.

Chapter Twenty

EZRA KINGSTON

I LEAVE ATHENA'S HOUSE and begin walking home with the kiss on my mind. I have been wanting to kiss her and feel her lips on mine for the longest time. She's truly the most beautiful girl I've ever seen.

With her blue ocean like eyes, midnight black hair, and full pink lips, she's gorgeous. I can't believe I never noticed her sooner, but I'm glad I did now.

She makes me feel things I've never felt before, not even with my first girlfriend. That kiss we shared made me feel more things than my whole one-year relationship with my ex-girlfriend, Avery.

She and I dated for a year, but we just lost feelings. We never had sex. We just shared kisses, cuddled, and went on dates, but over time we fell out of *love*.

I always told her I loved her, but in reality, didn't. When we broke up, it came out that we both didn't love each other. It was more of a friendly love. Our break up wasn't messy, it was mutual.

I feel so many different things with Athena. I feel happy, excited and nervous when I'm around her or just when I hear her name.

I walk down the sidewalk as the sun sets. Cars pass me as I continue walking down the cement sidewalk. I stick my hands in my hoodie pocket because they were starting to get cold.

The sun slowly goes down, making the sky turn orange and pink. Eventually, the sun is gone and the streetlights turn on.

I make it to the front door of my house and open it. Walking through, I close the door behind me. The house is empty yet again.

My mom is at work again. She works every night except Saturday and Sunday. Most of the time, I'm at home by myself, but when she is home we talk and catch up on things.

I walk upstairs to my bedroom and put my book bag on the floor. I walk to the bathroom and take my clothes off. Turning on the shower, I step in, feeling the warm water hit my chest and letting it slide down my muscles.

After my shower, I dry off and put on a pair of basketball shorts. It's around nine pm so I decide to lay in bed. My hands reach for my phone and I open Instagram. Scrolling through my feed, I come across a picture of Athena and her mother.

My thoughts soon drift to her again. The kiss we shared made me feel like my heart was going to explode with emotions. It felt like if she was in danger I would replace her with myself, which scares me. The kiss opened my eyes and helped me acknowledge my emotions I've been keeping locked away for so long when I'm with her.

I just want to protect her, know her, be near her, have her. I just want her. I don't know how she would react and I don't know if she feels the same way. I think I'm going to ask her to go on a date with me Sunday. She might say no and I don't know what that would do to me, but if she does, I won't give up.

She makes me happy. I make her happy. She makes me smile. I make her smile. She makes me feel things and I hope I make her feel things. She's one of the best things that's happened to me in a while.

She is perfect in my eyes. With that last thought in my mind, I slowly fall asleep.

Chapter Twenty-One

ATHENA LEWIS

THE NEXT MORNING I wake up with an actual smile on my face and a well-rested body. I didn't have a nightmare last night, so I got a full night's rest.

I was thinking a lot about the kiss before I fell asleep. The kiss Ezra and I shared made me feel things I felt with Zeke, feelings I've missed.

Ezra makes me happy. He makes me smile, laugh and sleep better. I love being around him. I think that I like him. I really don't know. It's been so long since I've felt romantic emotions. But he makes me happy and that's that.

If he doesn't feel the same way, I don't want me feeling this way to mess up our friendship.

Now at school, I'm at my metal locker, getting my laptop for English. When someone taps my shoulder, I spin around and come face to face with June.

"Hey, can I talk to you?" She asks, a small smile playing on her lips.

"Yeah, what's up?"

June looks around us and then back at me. "Come with me," she says and then grabs my hand, making me look at her in confusion..

June pulls me down the hallway, towards the Gymnasium. She pushes the door open and I gasp in surprise.

In the middle of the gym, Ezra is smiling and holding a sign that says, **Sunshine, will you go on a date with me Sunday?** In big bold letters.

June lets go of my arm and walks over to Summer, who kisses her head. June and Summer give me encouraging and happy smiles.

"Will you?" Ezra asks with a nervous smile on his face, looking extremely adorable. My heart stutters slightly as he runs his hand through his fluffy brown hair.

"Yes," I whisper, still slightly in shock. Ezra, still smiling, walks over to me and wraps his muscular arms around me, engulfing me with his scent. I slightly snuggle into his chest and then I wrap my arms around him. I like being in his arms. They make me feel safe. I haven't felt this sort of comfort in a while, a comfort I've missed.

Ezra and I are now in English and working on the essay once again. Ezra has been telling me jokes all throughout class. Every time I laugh his eyes become brighter, and shine with happiness.

"Why do we tell actors to break a leg?" He starts, telling me another one of his cheesy jokes.

I look at him and raise an arched eyebrow. "I don't know, why?"

"Because every play has a cast," he laughs with a proud smile on his face. Butterflies fly around my stomach as I look at how adorable he looks.

"That was very bad, wasn't it?" He asks before releasing a sigh. He places his head on his palm and then he stares at me, a sparkle in his emerald eyes.

"Yes, it was so bad it's funny," I giggle, shaking my head.

"Ezra and Athena stop messing around and get to work!" Mr. Wilson snaps. Ezra and I look at each other with wide eyes, but eventually, we get back to our classwork.

Today being Thursday, I just arrived at work and I walk to the back, grabbing the food that I need to deliver to a table. I balance the metal tray, that's holding the plates of food, on my palm and carefully make it to the table. "Here you go," I tell the elderly couple that's occupying the table.

"Thank you, dear," the elderly woman speaks, a motherly like smile on her wrinkled face and aged.

"You're welcome, ma'am. Enjoy," I nod with a real smile on my face. Her husband smiles at me and I leave them to eat their food.

My shift continues for two hours until Gina tells me I'm free to go. I'm thankful she let me go earlier than normal. I needed this because I need to visit someone.

I walk down the familiar gravel path for a little while. My feet stop and I sit on the dead grass, in front of the marble tombstone.

William Lewis

1977- 2007

Husband, father, and friend, taken too soon.

I place my hand on his tombstone and sigh. I look at the dead flowers and take them off of his tombstone. It's been so long since I've been here.

"Hi dad, it's been a while since I've talked to you. A lot of things have changed," I let out a breathy laugh, salty tears starting to escape, finally breaking free. "Ian turned seven months old a little while ago. I'm in my senior year now and I'm graduating soon," I stop to take a breath and wipe my tears away. "There is this boy in my class. His name is Ezra and he plays football. He makes me happy and I like him a lot. If you were still here, I'm sure you would like him too," I continue, blinking away the remainder of my tears, clearing my vision.

I talk to his tombstone until the sun goes down, my words flowing out of my mouth, not stopping until I've told him everything I wanted. I get up off of the cold ground and kiss my hand, placing it on the tombstone.

"I'll be back soon, dad. I love you," I whisper, my voice slightly cracking. My body shivers as a strong gust of blows through the cemetery, as if he's telling me he loves me too.

I leave the cemetery with unshed tears in my eyes. The last time I visited his tombstone was a few months after Ian was born. I know that he won't ever respond, but I like talking to him and filling him in on my life.

Wiping my tears away, I continue walking home, moving along the sidewalk and under the streetlights that create an orange glow.

Chapter Twenty-Two

EZRA KINGSTON

I**T'S SUNDAY AND ATHENA** and I's date is today. I would be lying if I said that I wasn't nervous because I'm a hundred percent nervous. *What if she doesn't like the place I chose? What if I say the wrong things?* Only Athena would make me this nervous.

The time is three-thirty pm and I told Athena I would walk to her house around four. Then we would walk to the ice cream shop. The ice cream shop is pretty close and I know she's terrified of cars, so I chose a place within walking distance.

When I make it to Athena's house, I raise my hand and knock on her door. On the other end of the door is shuffling and then the door opens. My mouth slightly opens as my eyes wander over Athena's face and body.

"You look," I breathe out. "Beautiful," I finish, making her cheeks tint a shade of pink.

Athena smiles at me. "Don't I always look beautiful?" She teases, a grin forming on her lips.

"Always," I whisper, my eyes meeting her sparkling blue ones.

She is wearing a pink half cut shirt, a black long fluffy skirt, black heeled boots, and neutral makeup. I don't think she needs makeup, she looks gorgeous even without it.

"Thank you," she blushes further. "And you look very handsome."

My cheeks slightly heat up. *How can she make me blush so much?*

Her blue eyes glimmer in the bright sunlight and she sticks her hand out, allowing me to lace out fingers together.

"So where are we going?" She asks as we start walking along the sidewalk. Her heeled boots click along the sidewalk with each step she takes.

"I was thinking about going to the ice cream shop that just opened," I inform her and Athena smiles, excitement all over her face.

"I haven't had ice cream in a long time," she mumbles with a slight laugh.

I send her a look of shock. "Why not?"

"I had to," she stops. "I've been busy," she mutters, looking at the ground as we continue walking. I nod, waiting for her to elaborate, but she doesn't and that's okay with me.

After a little more walking, we make it to the ice cream shop and tell the cashier what we want. I get Cookies & Cream and Athena gets Cotton Candy. We leave the ice cream shop after paying and decide to go down to the beach that's behind it and eat our ice cream there.

I glance at Athena and see that she has a little bit of ice cream on the side of her face. I grab a napkin and slowly start wiping the ice cream off of her face. I lean in closer to her face, my heart beating rapidly.

"What are you-" Athena says with surprise, but I silence her with my lips.

Athena gasps, but she kisses me back and I pull her to me by her waist, pressing our chests together. Her hands grip my hair and she moans as I press light kisses on her neck. She pulls away and her eyes shine with happiness, resembling the ocean in front of us.

Athena places her head on my shoulder and I wrap my arm around her waist. She sighs in content and I kiss her forehead lightly.

"I-," she starts, still looking at the ocean and watching as the waves lap against the shore. "I like you a lot, Ezra. You make me feel things I haven't felt in years. You make me a happy and better person. But there are things that I'm scared to tell you, things that may make you leave me. I don't want you to leave me," she whispers the last part, her soft voice shaking slightly.

"Sunshine, you don't have to tell me if you're not ready. You make me feel things I've never felt before too. I like the way you make me feel too. I have things I'm scared to tell you too and I won't leave you," I confess to her and she kisses me again. "I promise."

I cup her cheek and bring her closer to me. I kiss her slowly and passionately. Our lips move in sync, following one another's, our tongues massaging each other's as the sun dims in front of us.

We pull away and she places her head on my shoulder again and we watch as the sun goes down. I look over at her and see her smiling at me.

"Don't make promises you can't keep," she closes her eyes, her head still on my shoulder as the sun sets, the waves of the ocean lapping against the shore.

"I promise you, I'm keeping this one," I tell her, pulling her closer to me. My arms wrap around her waist and I lay my head on hers.

All I know is that I never want this moment to end.

Chapter Twenty-Three

ATHENA LEWIS

I LAUGH AS EZRA tells me another joke. Today being Tuesday, it's been about two days since our first date. The date went better than I expected. We got close, close enough for our lips to touch.

Ezra asked me out on another date after school today and I said yes. I like him and I'm not letting him get away just because I'm scared. But I am scared that he will find out about Ian. And if he does, I know that he'll leave me, even if he says that he won't.

Ezra and I are at my house and he drove here. He wanted to take me somewhere that's not in our town. The only problem is that it's two hours away and we have to drive, in a car. I said yes, but I'm not completely sure about it. *What if we crash and I lose Ezra?*

Ezra looks at me. "Ready to go?" He asks, a look of concern on his face as I pale.

My hands become clammy, nerves twisting in my stomach. "Y-yes."

He cups my face, his green eyes searching mine. "I will hold your hand and I'll drive slow. If you want to stop, I'll stop Athena, okay?" He reassures, pressing his forehead against mine. I nod against his forehead and close my eyes. Ezra kisses my forehead softly, making my nerves ease slightly.

We leave the house and I lock it behind us. I stare at his car for a couple of minutes and then, I grab the door handle with shaky hands. After a few moments, I pull it open and slowly get in. I tense when I sit in the seat and immediately grab the seatbelt, feeling some sort of comfort when it's on. Ezra looks at me with worry, but I give him a reassuring nod.

Ezra starts the car and grabs my hand. His thumb slowly massages my knuckles and I roll down the window, breathing in the fresh air.

Ezra stays true to his word, driving slow and occasionally pulling over to the side of the road when I get too scared. It takes us three and a half hours to get to our destination. When we pull in I almost cry at the sight.

He drove us to the Zoo. I haven't been here since I was five. The last time I was here I was with my dad. I kiss Ezra's cheek and he smiles at me.

"This is amazing, thank you."

"You're welcome, Sunshine."

"Ready to go in?" He asks, a happy and satisfied smile on his face. I nod excitedly, making him release a chuckle.

Deciding where to go first, I pick the wolves' habitat. Wolves are beautiful animals so I chose them first. I drag Ezra along with me and he laughs as I basically run over to the wolf enclosure.

"They are so pretty," I whisper, memorized by the white and grey wolf that's licking its pup.

"I know," Ezra whispers next to me. I look at him and see him already looking at me.

"That was so cheesy," I laugh, a huge smile on my face, making his cheeks turn a light shade of pink.

"I know, shush," he laughs with me, making me walk closer to him and place a soft and slow kiss on his lips.

★★★

Ezra is now driving back home and it's pretty dark out. My stomach tightens with nerves every time a car passes us in the opposite lane. The sun is almost down and suddenly Ezra stops on the side of the road, next to the woods. I look at him with confusion before he speaks.

"Put this on," he tells me and gives me a blindfold. "Trust me," he laughs and I take the cloth blindfold from him.

"If you kill me, I'll come back just to kill you."

"Athena, I'm not going to kill you." he laughs again.

I put the blindfold on and he helps me out of the car. Ezra grabs my hand and leads me to the woods. That's my guess at least. We continue walking for a little bit and then he lets go of my hand. I stand still for a couple of minutes and then take off the blindfold.

I look in front of me in confusion. In front of me is all lit up and there is a path with lights strung through the trees. I walk slowly and follow it until it ends.

When I make it to the end, my eyes fill with tears. Ezra is holding a bouquet of red roses underneath a gazebo and there are rose petals all over the floor. Behind him is a speaker with fairy lights flowing down, making it look like a wall of lights.

I walk over to him with a huge smile on my face and happy tears in my eyes.

He holds his hand out and places the roses on the railing. I take his hand. "Would you like to dance?"

"I would love to," I laugh, sniffling.

The music turns on and I look at him. Ezra places his hands on my waist and I link mine behind his head. I follow his movements as we dance into the night, laughing and smiling at one another. It feels as if I'm a princess in a Disney movie and he's my prince charming. Our lives are no fairy tale though.

Then suddenly the music stops and Ezra looks at me nervously. "Sunshine, you're the most beautiful girl I've seen. You understand me and me you. You don't push things on me and you're patient. Athena Lewis, would you do me the honor and be my girlfriend?" He asks, his voice shaking with the last sentence. I nod, a wide smile on my face, salty tears sliding down my face.

Oh my goodness! Yes!

"I would love you to be your girlfriend, Ezra Kingston," I answer with a giggle and his eyes glimmer with the familiar happiness. He leans down to capture my lips and I kiss him back, feeling a ton of emotions, happiness, excitement, and contentment.

Clapping and cheering is suddenly heard behind us. Pulling away, I spin around and gasp in a slight shock. My mom, another woman who I'm guessing is Ezra's mom, and June and Summer are behind us clapping and cheering with smiles on their faces.

"Finally!" My mother cheers and I laugh.

Ezra wraps his arm around my waist and we talk with everyone for a while. After some time, we clean up the woods and then head home. Ezra drives me home, his hand on my thigh the whole drive home. He pulls into my driveway and parks outside of my house.

He turns to me. "I'll see you tomorrow, Sunshine," he whispers leaning towards me, kissing my lips and I kiss him back

"Bye," I whisper back and then I exit the car.

From my spot on my porch, I wave at him. Unlocking the door with my copy of the house key, I enter the house and walk into the kitchen, filling a vase up with water and placing the roses in it.

I walk upstairs to my room and take a shower with one thought in my mind. *Who would have thought that Ezra Kingston would be my boyfriend?* Definitely not me, but I'm glad he is. He makes me happy.

Chapter Twenty-Four

EZRA KINGSTON

I T'S BEEN ABOUT TWO weeks since I asked Athena to be my girlfriend. It's the best decision I've ever made. Things have been going great, but Stacy came back last week.

Athena smiles at me when I walk over to her and kiss her on the lips. I pull away, allowing her to close her locker. She reaches for my hand and I place mine in hers, lacing our fingers together. We walk down the hallway, talking quietly to one another.

We pass Stacy on the way to the cafeteria and she sends me a glare and then she smirks, like she knows something I don't. I turn my attention to Athena who looks at me in confusion, my expression matching hers. I shrug in response to her questioning look.

"What was that about?" She asks, watching Stacy's retreating figure.

I rub my thumb over her knuckles. "No idea," I mumble just as confused.

When we make it to the lunchroom, I grab us a seat and we sit down at the table. Athena sits in the chair next to me and I wrap my arm around her waist. She releases a small sigh, letting me know she's comfortable.

"You're so cute," she mumbles, adoringly and I look at her with a slightly heated face.

"And you're gorgeous," I mumble into her ear and place a soft kiss on her neck, making her blue eyes flutter closed.

"Ezra, I swear to god if you keep doing that I'm going t-" she's interrupted by her soft moan when I press a kiss to her neck again. "Damn you."

She looks at me with lust in her eyes. "Not here, Ezra," she groans, tilting her head to the side and I halt my movements, knowing not to piss her off.

"Can I have your attention!" A familiar voice shouts, making Athena and I turn to look at Stacy along with the rest of the teenagers in the cafeteria.

The whole cafeteria quiets down and Stacy smirks proudly, thinking she's the queen or something. She clears her throat and begins to talk.

"Did any of you know that little Ms. Nerd isn't as innocent as you think? Well, I didn't until about a week ago!" She shouts, luring people into what she has to say. She claps her hands and continues.

I look at Athena, who now has a pale face. She has her eyes locked on Stacy, who is now staring at her, fake pity on her face.

"N-No," Athena whispers to herself.

"Yeah remember her previous boyfriend, Zeke? Athena is a dirty whore and spreads her legs for anyone!" Stacy shouts, her cold eyes taunting my girlfriend.

"Get to the point bitch!" Someone shouts, making Stacy stomp her foot and roll her blue eyes.

"What I'm trying to say is, Athena Lewis has a kid!" She finishes, a satisfied smile on her face. I look at Stacy in shock, along with the rest of the people in the cafeteria. "Yeah, a son! He's seven months old and she named him after Zeke!"

Whispers of disbelief erupt from teenagers. Many of them point and laugh at Athena, gossiping amongst themselves.

"Why didn't you tell me?" Emily walks over to us, shouting at Athena, who is choking on her tears.

"I," she starts, but stops to look at me.

I stare at my girlfriend, who is shaking with tears in her eyes. She looks at me with guilt swimming in her eyes. *It's true? This is her secret?*

"Ezra, I-" Athena stutters, but is interrupted by Stacy.

"Here I have proof!" Stacy shouts and grabs pictures out of her bag. I look at them and my heart shatters. It's true. They're pictures of Athena smiling and laughing with a little boy that has blue eyes and brown hair. *Her blue eyes.*

"I can't believe I was in love with you!" Stacy screams at Athena, making my eyes grow even wider. "Skank!"

June and Summer walk over to us quickly with panic on their faces. It's now that I look down at my girlfriend again. She's shaking and breathing quickly. She's having a panic attack.

"Ezra, take her home. I'll shut that bitch up," Summer says with worry and turns towards Stacy with a pissed off look on her face.

"Athena, baby. Sunshine, look at me, breathe. You're okay." I say with my voice cracking, a few tears in my eyes, the feeling of betrayal evident. Her breathing slowly returns to normal and I pull her to me. I need to get her out of here, especially away from judgmental eyes.

Mr. Baxter walks into the cafeteria, a few other teachers following him, and I groan. "What's going on in here?" The chatter stops and I don't wait for him to continue, instead I leave the cafeteria, carrying Athena in my arms.

"Skank!"

"Slut!"

"Whore!"

Those words are thrown at Athena as I carry her out of the school. I place her in my car and I drive to her house. There is no way I'm taking her to my house.

I grab her house key from her bag and unlock the door. I go back to the car and pick her up. She wraps her arms around my neck and snuggles into me. I kiss her forehead and place her on the couch.

I grab the blanket that's on the back of the couch and drape it over her. I kiss her forehead again and sit on the floor next to her.

"I'm sorry," she whispers, her eyes fluttering closed. I hold one of her hands, caressing it gently.

Now I understand why she was worried about me leaving her, hell I would be too. Having a son at a young age is a big thing to be scared to tell someone about, especially your boyfriend.

I'm glad that I finally know. I just wish she was the one to tell me. I feel a little disappointed that she has a son and he's not mine, but I can't change that. What's done is done.

I watch as my beautiful girlfriend sleeps quietly on the couch. I want her to tell me everything from start to finish. I will tell her my secret when I'm ready. I think it's finally time I tell someone and that's going to be her. A step forward in our relationship.

I hope she doesn't think I'm going to leave her because I'm not and that's for damn sure. I like her too much and I care for her too much. She's a big piece of my heart now. I run my fingers through her hair and kiss her forehead and then I press my lips to each knuckle on her warm hand.

Chapter Twenty-Five

EZRA KINGSTON

A THENA SHIFTS ON THE couch, but she remains asleep. I continue to run my fingers through her soft hair and then I cup her cheek to run my thumb across her soft bottom lip.

She whimpers in her sleep, making me move my hand back to her cheek, letting her snuggle into it again. I smile at her. I can't believe I got so lucky, being able to call this strong and beautiful woman mine is the best feeling ever.

I close my eyes and lean back against the couch while I wait for Athena to wake up. I'm definitely not waking her up. She needs some sleep after what happened.

Athena stirs and slowly sits up on the couch. She rubs her eyes and looks at me with guilt written on her face. "Ezra, I'm so sorry," she whispers with tears in her eyes.

"Baby, it's okay. I just wish you were the one to tell me," I whisper back to her.

"I was too scared. I thought t-that you would leave me. Please don't leave," she sobs, tears falling down her beautiful face. "I'm sorry."

I sit on the couch next to her and pull her into my arms. Her body shakes as she sobs into my shoulder. "Sunshine, I'm not leaving you ever, I promise," I reassure her while I rub her back.

She pulls away and my hands rest on her waist. I look into her eyes that now have a red rim around them from crying. "You're not?"

"Of course not," I place a small kiss on her lips, my fingers holding the back of her neck to bring her closer to me.

"Are you hungry?" I ask her since we didn't get to eat our lunch. Her stomach grumbles and she lets out a sniffle and a small laugh.

"Yes I am," she wipes the tears off of her face. Athena climbs off of me and we go to the kitchen. I look through the fridge and then pick out stuff for sandwiches.

We eat in silence and suddenly Athena speaks. "I had Ian about seven months ago," I stop eating and stare at her, her eyes now burning into the wooden table in front of us.

"After the car crash, I was in a state of depression and I wouldn't eat or move. My mom sent me to Ohio for therapy and to keep my pregnancy a secret, because the Colt family completely turned against me after Zeke passed away," she sniffles, pausing to wipe a stray tear away.

"When I had Ian, he was my light in life. He made me happy, but I couldn't always be a mother to him. So, I placed him with a family friend," she continues, her eyes now looking into mine.

I kiss her on the lips and then she snuggles into the crook of my neck, her breathing sending shivers through my body. "Thank you for telling me," I whisper into her ear and kiss her neck softly.

She moans in response. "You're welcome," she pulls away and then kisses me hungrily.

"I want you," she whispers, biting her lip seductively, making my eyes immediately. I've never had sex with anyone and this is all new to me.

"I-I'm a virgin," I stutter with tinted cheeks. Athena looks at me and traces her thumb on my bottom lip.

"We don't have to if you don't want to," she reassures me quickly. "Ezra, we don't."

"Athena, I want to. I want you," I tell her, making her smile. I stand up off the chair and Athena wraps her legs around my waist.

I quickly walk us up the stairs. "Door on the right," she mumbles, pulling away for a slight second before continuing to kiss my lips.

I push open her door and lock it behind us. Walking over to the bed, I lay her on it, me hovering over her.

ATHENA LEWIS

Ezra hovers over me, both of us kissing one another while we fight for dominance. Ezra takes off my shirt and then my pants, leaving me in my gray lace panties. My fingers grip the hem of his t-shirt and I quickly pull it off of him, wanting to see his muscular chest.

He stands up to take off his pants, his belt first, and then his pants. He hovers over me again, only in his boxers. "Athena," he whispers nervously against my lips. "I've never gone farther than this," he looks into my eyes.

"It's okay," I reassure him, placing one of my hands on his face. "I'm here with you. We'll go at your pace," I whisper and Ezra nods against my forehead.

He strips out of his boxers and kicks them onto the floor. "Is this okay?" I ask as I trail my hands down his chest, moving lower and lower until I stop above his hard and erect length.

"Yes. It's more than okay," he breathes out, his chest moving up and down rapidly.

"I want you," he murmurs against my lips. "Now."

I grab his hand and place it on the top of my lace underwear, making Ezra look at me hesitantly. "It's okay. Remember, only if you want to," I remind him and he nods.

Hooking his fingers into my underwear, Ezra drags them down my legs, leaving my lower half bare in front of him. When my underwear is off and somewhere on the floor, Ezra removes my lace bra from my chest as I guide him. My face slightly heats up as I'm fully exposed to my boyfriend.

I grab Ezra's hand and I guide it towards my wet core. When his fingers make contact with my swollen bud, my toes curl and I release a small moan.

"Just move your fingers in a circle," I explain, helping him for a few moments until he gets a rhythm going.

"Like this?" He asks, unsure. "I don't want to hurt you."

"Yes, and Ezra, you won't hurt me," I gasp, my fingers gripping the sheet beneath us as he moves his fingers faster.

"Shit," I pant, my toes curling as my climax nears. I pull Ezra down for a deep kiss, my body reaching its peak, waves of pleasure washing over my sweaty body.

Bringing Ezra down for another kiss, I moan as his hard length presses against my core and I quickly pull away.

"Is something wrong?"

"We need a condom," I rush out.

"Right," he says as he picks his pants up off of the floor and grabs his wallet, pulling a foil packet out and dropping his pants onto the floor.

Hovering over me again, Ezra holds the open rubber condom. Unsure of what to do, he looks at me, his green eyes nervous.

"Do you want me to put it on you?" I ask him softly, noticing how he doesn't move to roll the condom on.

"Y-yes."

I take the condom from him and lower my hand towards his length. My hand touches the tip of it, making Ezra shudder and release a soft gasp. I roll the condom onto his length, biting my lip as *he* throbs in my hand.

"Athena," he gasps, his length growing harder every second that it's in my warm hand.

"Are you sure, Ezra?"

"Positive," he whispers, looking at me with so much raw emotion.

I position Ezra's cock at my warm entrance and then, I allow him to ease his way in, his hips stuttering as he enters me more and more. I release encouraging moans along the way, enough to tell him how good he's doing. Trust me, he's amazing already.

I gasp as his cock enters me fully. Slowly, he begins thrusting into me, grunting and moaning lowly. "Ezra, don't try to be good. Just be here, with me, you and I."

I thread my fingers through his hair and lower his head to the crook of my neck, allowing him to suck on the soft skin there as he thrusts into me. I wrap my legs around his waist, pushing him deeper inside of me.

We move together slowly, but gradually picking up speed. Us, two people longing for the other, us, together.

"I'm close," I pant, my teeth grazing his shoulder, him moving in and out of me at a steady pace. My legs lock around him as my orgasm flows through my body. My eyes roll back into my head as he continues to thrust into me.

"Fuck!" I hiss, my teeth sinking into my bottom lip.

Ezra stills, his body tense. He releases a few moans before his body twitches, his orgasm flowing through his own body. He pants and releases another moan before he lays on top of me. His sweaty chest against my own.

"That was," he trails off, still panting.

"Amazing," I finish his sentence, my fingers in his hair as he lays his head on my stomach.

"It was the best experience I've ever had. Romantically," he speaks, his fingers caressing the side of my stomach. "You're so beautiful," he mumbles against my stomach.

"Ezra," I whisper, my eyes locked onto his hair. "I like you so much and I-I'm afraid of losing you," I confess to him while I'm in my most vulnerable state.

"You won't lose me, Athena," he turns his head, looking me in the eyes. "Don't think like that."

Eventually, Ezra pulls out of me and throws away the condom in the garbage can that's in my bathroom. Ezra and I snuggle in bed with each other for a little while and then we get up to take a shower, together.

Chapter Twenty-Six

ATHENA LEWIS

I BASICALLY FLOAT DOWN THE stairs the next morning and see my mom cooking breakfast. A smile forms on my lips and I walk over to her.

She pauses what she's doing and pulls me into a hug. "Do you work today?"

"Yes, and after, Ezra and I are probably going to hang out here," I reply and pull away from the hug, glancing at the food she's making.

She smiles softly. "I'm glad you found someone who makes you happy, seeing you smile is the best thing I've seen in a while."

"I'm glad I found him too."

"Hungry?" She asks as she flips the pancakes in the pan. I nod quickly, starving after yesterday's *activities* with Ezra.

I take a seat at the table and she places my plate of food in front of me. We eat our breakfast, talking occasionally. Ezra is picking me up in fifteen minutes, so I only have a little time to eat.

A knock on the door is heard a little after I finish eating my breakfast.

Gripping the door knob and pulling it open with a smile on my face, it soon drops when I see Ezra with a bloody nose and a busted lip.

I quickly help him sit on the couch. "What the hell happened? And don't say you got jumped again!" I shout at him, not because I'm angry, but because I'm worried.

"I need a rag and ice," he mumbles, his eyes staring at the ground, completely ignoring my question. "I'll tell you soon," he whispers.

I rush to the kitchen to get ice and a rag, slamming drawers shut and wetting the rag in the process. Walking back into the living room quickly, I sit next to him and start to wipe the blood away.

"Oh my goodness, what happened?" My mom asks with wide eyes when she comes into the living room.

I glance at her and give her a shrug. "I got it, mom. Could you get me another rag?"

"I'll be right back," she rushes out of the room.

I cup his cheek and carefully place the ice on his lip. "Who did this to you?" I ask, wanting to know who hurt my boyfriend. Ezra remains quiet.

My mom walks back into the living room and gives me a towel. "I'll leave you two be," she exits the room again, leaving Ezra and I by ourselves while I tend to his wounds.

I stare at Ezra and rub my thumb across his cheek slowly. "Please tell me," I whisper, my voice cracking with each word.

He closes his eyes and sighs, and eventually, he lets his guard down, revealing his secret to me. "My father."

I look at him with tears in my eyes. *How could his own father do this to him?* That's not a father anymore, that's the scum of the earth.

"He's an alcoholic. My mom kicked him out a little while ago and he turned up this morning asking us for money. I told him no several times and he punched me in the face. My mom called the cops on him and he got arrested," he continues and a tear rolls down his cheek, making me wipe it away, not wanting to see him cry. "I needed to see you. I'm sorry."

"Don't you dare apologize," I whisper and look into his forest-like eyes. "I'm so sorry you had to go through that. I-I can't even imagine."

He pulls me into his chest and I lay my head on it, listening to his heartbeat. "We have school," I tell him while trying to pull myself out of his hold, but enjoying his company.

"We'll go in late," he mumbles and puts his head in the crook of my neck. I snuggle into him, welcoming his warmth and touch.

Ezra and I are now at lunch and we are sitting with June and Summer. I was pretty nervous to come to school today because everyone knows that I have a son. I'm glad that Ezra didn't leave me. I don't know what would happen if he did.

Nobody really said anything to me, except this one jock named John. He called me a whore, but Ezra told him to fuck off and pretty much embarrassed him in front of a crowd of people.

Mr. Baxter told me this morning that Stacy was expelled and that her parents sent her to a boarding school in California. It's close to the end of the school year, so I don't know why they would put her back in school, but I couldn't care less.

I laugh at another cheesy joke Ezra makes, making his eyes light up when I laugh or smile. I'm still pissed at what his dad did to him. I would love to punch that asshole myself. If you hurt my boyfriend, someone I care about, I'll hurt you.

The lunch bell rings and we throw away our trash. Ezra and I hold hands as we leave the cafeteria. "You're so gorgeous," Ezra murmurs in my ear. His breath fans my neck, making my eyes flutter closed.

"Not here," I mumble sternly. He chuckles and kisses my cheek as an alternative.

We continue walking down the hallway until Emily walks in front of us, a look of desperation on her face. "Can I help you?"

"Can we please talk? Just two minutes is all I'm asking for."

"Fine. Two minutes, that's all."

Ezra looks at me with worry on his face. "I'll see you after school," I reassure him. He nods and kisses my cheek, sending me one last look before walking away.

"Okay, I know I hurt you emotionally and physically, but I'm so sorry, Athena. I was blinded by rage and I let my emotions get in the way of our friendship. Can we please be friends again?" She begs, tears forming in her familiar eyes. "I miss our friendship."

"Even though I miss you a lot, you hurt me. I've cried myself to sleep because of you. I've thought about ending my life because of you. We can be friends, but we will never be as close as we were before. I'm sorry," I tell her, tears in my own eyes.

"I understand," she nods, wiping a few tears away.

"I'm glad you do," I reply and turn away to leave.

"Oh, and Athena?" She asks, making me stop in my tracks and turn around to look at her "I'm happy for you. You're probably a great mother to your little boy."

"Thank you," I whisper to her before walking away, wiping my tears away as I walk down the hallway to my next class.

Forgive, but never forget.

Chapter Twenty-Seven

EZRA KINGSTON

ATHENA AND I HOLD hands as we walk out of school together. She has work in a couple of hours, so we are going to hang out at her house. Since I'll already be at her house, I'm dropping her off at work.

We walk to my car and get in. I close my door and put on my seatbelt. I then turn on the radio. Athena closes her door and puts her seatbelt on too. Putting the key in the ignition I start the car and hand on Athena's thigh. She gives me a look and I give her an innocent smile.

I pull out of the parking lot and turn on to the main road. "Sunshine?"

"Yes?" She replies quietly.

"When you go to visit Ian on Sunday, can I come with you?" I ask, hesitantly. When she turns to look at me, my eyes look before I turn my attention back to the road.

Athena stays quiet for a little while and I start to panic a little bit. "Of course," she whispers.

"Really?" I ask in surprise and my stomach blossoms with excitement. *Should I bring him some toys, or would that be weird?*

"Yes, really. I'd love for you to meet him."

I turn onto Athena's street and continue driving until I make it to her house. Pulling into her driveway, I park the car and get out. Athena follows me and she unlocks her door and I follow her in. Closing the door behind us, I kick off my shoes and put them on the shoe rack.

Athena sits on the couch with a sigh and looks at me with a warm smile. She holds her arms out, welcoming me to her. "Can we cuddle?"

I nod quickly, wanting nothing more than to hold her. I walk over to the couch and sit down, effortlessly pulling her into my chest, both of us laying down, comfortable in each other's arms.

Athena looks at me with sparkling blue eyes and a warm smile on her full lips. "I know that you're not Ian's biological father and I definitely don't want to pressure you with that role in his life just because you're my boyfriend."

I look at her with a frown and scrunched eyebrows. "I know that I will never be his biological father, but I will try my hardest to fill that role in his life. I want nothing more than to make you happy, Athena Marie Lewis," I cup her cheek and trace my thumb over her bottom lip.

"You have gone through so much. You deserve to be happy, to smile and laugh, to be able to sleep without having nightmares. And to go to school without being embarrassed or exposed," kiss her on the lips slowly. "You deserve the world, beautiful," I continue and wipe away the tear that's rolling down her cheek.

"You make me a happy person. You make me sleep better, Ezra. I'm so happy I have you in my life and I'm glad that Ian will have someone so kind and sweet like you. You have gone through so much as well. You deserve the world as much you say I do," she murmurs, pulling me down for a slow kiss.

"I already have everything I want," I whisper and lay my head in the crook of her neck, breathing in her scent.

I pull into the crowded parking lot of Gina's café and park. I look at Athena, pouting because I don't want her to leave. "Be careful, Sunshine. Oh, and I'm picking you up after work."

"Thank you, but you don't have to."

"Too bad I am," I insist, playfully. She giggles and kisses my lips. I kiss her back and kiss her cheek after she pulls away.

"Be safe," I say quickly before she gets out of the car, watching as a few cars drive by.

"Yes, sir," she winks playfully and walks into the café. I shake my head with a small smirk on my face. This woman knows what she's doing to me. She has me completely wrapped around her finger.

I start my car and pull out of the parking lot and onto the main road. I turn on my radio and sing along, tapping my thumb against the steering wheel to match the beat.

I drive down the familiar roads that take me to my house. My mom is home today since I'm pretty sure she took today off. So, while Athena is at work, she and I are going to spend some time together.

I pull into the driveway and park my car next to my mom's. I get out and walk to the front door, unlocking it I walk inside and close the door behind me.

"Mom, I'm home!" I call out, kicking off my shoes.

"In the kitchen!" Her voice calls back.

I walk to the kitchen and stop in my tracks. "What the hell is he doing here?"

My father is sitting at our kitchen table and my mother releases a sigh. Her brown eyes dart between my father and I as she tucks a strand of her long dark brown hair behind her ear. "He is going to a treatment center to get help and he wanted to apologize to us, Ezra."

I slightly smile. Even though I'm pissed at him for what he's put us through, I'm glad that he's finally getting help. "I'm happy for you."

"Thank you, Ezzie," he smiles, using his nickname for me, tears in his green eyes. "I'm so sorry for what I put you two through," he looks at my mom and me, wiping his tears away.

"I know you are," I reply, placing a hand on his shoulder before I leave the kitchen and go upstairs to my room. Taking a seat on my bed, I start to think.

My father and I were never really close, but it still hurts to know that he never made an effort to go to at least one of my football games. But now I'm glad that he is getting help, finally making a good decision.

Pulling onto the main road since I'm on my way to pick up Athena, I turn on my windshield wipers. It started raining a little while ago. The rain hits my car like it's being pelted with small pebbles, making it hard for me to see the busy road in front of me. A few cars pull off to the side of the road as the rain starts to come down harder, making it almost impossible to see now.

Just as I go through the intersection, bright lights speed towards me and I freeze with wide eyes, my blood running cold as my heart rate accelerates. The loud beeping of a horn is heard and then the loud bang of impact. My body jerks and my head hits my window, darkness invading my vision as a warm liquid drips down my forehead.

Chapter Twenty-Eight

ATHENA LEWIS

I PLACE A PLATE of hot food in front of some customers and grab their cups to refill their drinks. I walk away from their table and balance the cups on the metal tray.

I fill the cups with ice and then pour the water into them from the pitcher. I walk back to the table and set down the cups of water. I walk away from the table happily when I realize my shift is almost over and I can see my boyfriend soon.

When I walk into the back room, my phone starts ringing. I smile when I see that it's Ezra's mom, Sylvia, calling. "Hello?"

"Athena, I'm coming to pick you up from work. We have to go to the hospital. Ezra has been in a car accident." Those last words make my heart stop. I freeze and my eyes fill up with tears. *No. No. No.*

"Is he ok?" I ask her, frantically. My hands shake and my heart slams violently against my rib cage. *Pull yourself together, Athena.* I start to calm down, realizing I need to be strong for him. I have to be.

"I don't know at the moment," she replies, her sniffles telling me she's as worried as I am. "I'm here."

I hang up the phone and tell Gina goodbye. I run out of the café and get into Sylvia's car. I sit there silently and my hands shake on the way to the hospital. I bite my lip anxiously. *I can't lose him too* and with that in my mind, I start preparing myself for the worst.

"I can't lose him," I whisper to myself, trying to hold back my tears. My eyes follow the raindrops that slide down the glass window, matching the ones that are sliding down my face.

"Ezra Kingston," Sylvia tells the receptionist.

"Are you family?"

"Yes, I'm his mother and she is his girlfriend," Sylvia nods at me, her hands shaking by her side.

"His room number is 310, but only immediate family is alo-" the receptionist looks at me and is cut off by Sylvia.

"They have a child together," she snaps. "Is that family enough for you?"

"Let me check with my supervisor."

"Tell your supervisor to kiss my ass," Sylvia grabs my hand and we rush down the hallway.

Slyvia and I rush to Ezra's hospital room after the lady at the front desk tells us it. I, however, am pretty much running down the hallway frantically looking for his room number.

302. *No.*

304. *No, dammit.*

306. *No, shit.*

308. *No. Where is he?*

310. *Finally.*

I stand outside of the door, breathing heavily and Sylvia grabs my hand and we go in together.

I slowly walk into the room, my eyes filling up with warm tears. I let out a gasp as I look at Ezra's face. Ezra has a cut on his forehead and blood on his shirt. He's wide awake with a frown on his face.

"I'm not that ugly am I?" He jokes, looking at me with tears in his own eyes.

"Ezra," I whisper, ignoring his joke.

"Hi," he whispers back, realizing that his joke isn't funny at a time like this. I walk over and quickly hug him.

"I thought I lost you," I sob into his shirt. "I don't want to lose you, ever."

He pulls me on the bed with him and I lay my head on his chest. "You can't get rid of me that easily," he smirks and kisses my lips.

Sylvia clears her throat. "I'll give you two some time," she says with a relieved smile on her face and leaves the room.

I look at him with watery eyes. "How did it even happen?"

He sighs and stares into my eyes. "I was on my way to pick you up and I was driving through an intersection and it was raining hard. I could barely see anything and a car ran the light and crashed into the front side of my car," he explains, his larger hand gripping mine.

"I'm so sorry," I murmur and kiss him again. He pulls me closer to him and we lay there for a while, enjoying each other's comfort.

"It's not your fault, Sunshine," he mumbles after a little while. I open my mouth to argue, but he sends me a sharp look and I sigh, admitting that he's right.

The doctor soon walks in with a friendly smile on her face. She grabs a pen out of her white lab coat and looks over the chart she has in her hand. "Glad to see you're awake."

Ezra smiles at her and I narrow my eyes at the doctor. "Well, your injuries are minor. You may have a concussion from hitting your head on the window, and the gash on your forehead will heal eventually, but it may scar. I would say you are very lucky," she looks at us, glancing at Ezra and then me as she speaks. "You can be out of here in two hours."

"Thank you," Ezra tells her, and I nod at the doctor.

"You're very welcome," she replies before leaving the room.

I look at Ezra, but see him already looking at me with a smirk on his face "You're jealous."

"I am not," I defend, knowing damn well I am.

"Tell that to the glare you had on your face," he whispers teasingly.

I roll my eyes and snuggle into him. "Be quiet," I mumble against his chest. He chuckles and kisses my forehead softly.

"I'm glad you're okay," I whisper to him.

"I am too," he whispers back and lays his head on mine.

I close my eyes and think about how I enjoy being in his muscled arms. Slowly, I start to fall asleep in his warm and comforting embrace.

Chapter Twenty-Nine

ATHENA LEWIS

"BABY, WAKE UP," a deep voice whispers while shaking me awake. I groan and pout, not wanting to wake up yet. The person laughs quietly and my eyes snap open. I meet the green eyes of Ezra and I smile. He is standing next to the hospital bed, leaning over me and his mom is looking at us with a soft smile on her face. "Come on, it's time to go," he says.

Yawning with a stretch, I slowly climb out of the hospital bed. Ezra grabs my hand and we walk out of the hospital together. We all pile into the car and I sit in the back with Ezra, while Sylvia drives.

I lay my head on Ezra's shoulder and he rubs his thumb over my knuckles. "The doctor said that the cut on my forehead is going to scar, are you sure you still want to be with me?"

I jab my finger into his chest and look at him in disbelief. "Of course I still want to be with you!" I shout. What a dumb question to ask, especially right now. "I'm not going to leave you just because of one stupid and tiny scar!"

"Okay, okay, I'm sorry," he laughs while watching me in amusement.

"It's not funny," I mumble and he places a quick kiss on my lips.

"I like seeing you pissed. It makes you look hot as hell," he murmurs, huskily, against my lips, his green eyes staring at me, watching as I pull my bottom lip in between my teeth. My breath gets caught in my throat and I stare at him, squeezing my legs together. *Oh, fuck me.*

I clear my throat and pull my eyes away from him. "You hit your head too hard."

"That is true, but I'm just stating facts."

"Goodnight, Sunshine," Ezra gives me a goodnight kiss on the forehead.

"Goodnight, Ezra," I kiss him on the lips and then pull away from him, despite wanting to be in his arms all night.

"Bye, Sylvia. Thank you for the ride," I thank her with a grateful smile on my face. I open the car door and get out, my feet making contact with my gravel driveway.

"Of course. Be safe, Athena."

"I will," I close the car door and stand back. I wave them goodbye as they pull out of my driveway. When they're gone, I turn around and walk towards the front door. Unlocking it, I open it and walk through the threshold.

"Athena Marie Lewis!"

I jump, slightly startled and turn to my right and see my sitting on the couch with a book on her lap. She stands up and storms over to me.

"Hi, mom," I cringe with a small wave. *Shit.*

"That's all you have to say to me?"

"No," I shake my head. "I'm sorry. I was at work and Ezra was supposed to pick me up, but he got in a car accident and I forgot to call you," I explain frantically, trying not to dig a deeper hole for myself.

"Oh, my," she covers her mouth with her hands. "Is he alright?" She asks with a worried expression.

"Yes," I rub my face. "Thankfully, his injuries are minor and he'll live."

"He's a strong young man. He has to be to put up with you," she jokes before pulling me into a hug, a hug I really needed tonight. I lay my head on her shoulder and close my eyes. "You should get some sleep."

"I'm going right now," I pull away from the hug and kiss her on the forehead. "Goodnight, mom."

"Goodnight, sweetie."

If these past hours have made me realize something, it's that I never want to lose Ezra Kingston.

I yawn and tighten my hold on Ezra's hand. Right now we are in English and I'm extremely tired. I didn't go to bed until very late last night. I was up worrying about Ezra. My mind wouldn't calm down.

"How come you're so tired?" Ezra asks with concern.

"I went to bed late,," I reply after yawning for the third time.

I lay my head on his shoulder and close my eyes. "You're comfortable," I mumble, sleepily.

"I'm glad," he murmurs, kissing my head and then going back to work.

The ticking of the clock slowly lures me to sleep. Ezra's thumb traces circles on my thigh, making me slowly drift off, my mind finally calming down.

"Athena get up and do your work!" I jump as Mr. Wilson shouts at me. I roll my eyes. We only have five minutes left of class. *Let me sleep, damn.*

"Dick," Ezra mumbles under his breath. He wraps his arms around my waist and pulls me closer to him, making the metal chair screech against the tiled floor.

The bell soon rings, dismissing us and I pack up my books and papers. After I'm done grabbing my things, Ezra grabs my hand as we walk out of class together.

"Slut!" John, another football player, shouts at me from down the hall. His group of friends pat him on the back, encouraging him to continue. "Cum dumpster!"

The smile on my face slowly fades away and tears form in my eyes. I look at Ezra, who now has fury shown on his face. His hands are clenched at his sides while a muscle in his jaw ticks. "Ezra, don't!" I shout as he pulls his hand out of my hold.

He stomps over to John, who now has a pale face while his body shakes like a leaf in the wind. "Don't you even dare call her that! She is definitely not a slut! You're the one dating a female who spreads her legs for anyone!" Ezra shouts in his face, making the jock shrink back. Even though he's pissed, Ezra's still respectful to John's girlfriend, who's a cheating bitch.

He pushes John into the lockers making him fall. For a football player, John really isn't strong. John gets up with the help of his friends that pat him on the back again. A crowd of nosy students starts to form around them, most of them chanting, "Fight, fight, fight!"

Ezra storms over to me and grabs my hand. We turn to leave, but John decides to say something else. "She still has a kid! She's a dirty whore, man!"

Ezra charges at him and punches him in the face. Ezra only punches him once, but it's enough to leave John with a bloody nose and teary eyes. "I'm not your friend, *man*. Talk shit about my girlfriend again and see what happens!" He shouts, his face red with rage. I bite my lip, nervously.

Ezra walks over to me and grabs my hand. He pulls me down the hall with him and when we round a corner, he pushes me up against the lockers, picking me up and making me wrap my legs around his waist.

"You're mine, Athena. Mine," he declares, kissing me deeply against the lockers, me gasping as he bites my lip and tugs on it, pulling it towards him. "Whose are you?"

"Yours," I moan, biting my lip to stifle a moan.

"Damn right you are," he pulls away and looks into my eyes.

"We have to get to class," I tell him. He groans and kisses me on the lips slowly, teasing me. I narrow my eyes at him and all he does is smile innocently. He unwraps my legs from around his waist and I stand against him.

"I'll see you at lunch, handsome," I look up at him, a smile sitting on my lips.

"I'll see you there, beautiful," he grins and looks down at me with adoration in his eyes.

Our height difference is annoying. Ezra stands at six feet, while I'm five-foot-eight.

"Bye," I wink and pull away from him. His deep laugh is heard behind me as I walk away from him and down the hall towards my next class, History.

Chapter Thirty

ATHENA LEWIS

"**A**RE YOU READY?" I ask Ezra while I nibble on my bottom lip anxiously, waiting for his response. Today is Sunday and Ezra is meeting Ian for the first time. I'm worried that Ezra is going to change his mind about being with me and being a father figure to Ian.

Ezra sighs. "Sunshine, stop worrying. I already told you that I'm not leaving you, ever," he tells me with sincerity, his green eyes shining with happiness. "I promise."

"I-I," I start, but Ezra presses his lips to mine and starts kissing me slowly. He then pulls me closer to him by grabbing my waist and I wrap my arms around his neck, pressing my body against him so that there is no space left between us. Absolutely none.

I pull away and rest my forehead against his. "You're mine," he mumbles huskily.

"I'm yours," I whisper back breathlessly.

"Ezra, we have to go," I mumble, trying to pull away from him, but he tightens his hold on my waist and kisses my cheek softly.

"Fine, fine."

He finally lets go of me and I reach for his hand. Together we walk out of my house and get inside his mom's car. Ezra turns on the radio and pulls out of the driveway. He places one hand on my thigh and the other on the steering wheel. I sigh in content and place my hand on top of his.

Ezra's car is in the auto shop getting fixed. The right side of his car was completely smashed up and the windshield was a little shattered. I almost started crying when I saw the car.

The GPS that sits on the dashboard directs Ezra to our destination, Annalise and Lee's small house.

When we arrive, Ezra parks in the driveway and my stomach tightens with nerves. I slowly reach for the door handle and effortlessly climb out of the car. I close the door behind me and Ezra takes my hand in his when he walks over to me. The gravel and small rocks crunch beneath our shoes as we walk towards the front door of Annalise and Lee's house.

I raise my hand up and knock on the door, stepping back when I hear shuffling on the other side. The door opens and I come face to face with Annalise. "Hey, guys, come on in," she says with a warm smile on her face.

"Hey," I greet her and walk through the threshold with Ezra following close behind me.

"Hey, I'm Ezra," Ezra shakes Annalise's hand, but she pulls him into a hug.

"It's nice to finally meet you," Annalise smiles at him.

"You too," Ezra smiles back.

She leads us to the living room where Lee is sitting on the couch, watching TV, while Ian is playing with his toys on the floor.

"Hi, I'm Ezra," Ezra shakes Lee's hand when Lee stands. "It's nice to meet you."

"Likewise," Lee pats his soulder

I walk over to Ian with a smile on my face. "Hi, honey," I say and sit down on the floor next to him. His eyes light up and he giggles, slowly standing up to walk to me, wobbling with each small step.

I hold my arms out and pull him to me when he's close enough. "Mama, hi," he giggles and claps his small hands.

"Hi," I say again with a smile on my face. I look over at Ezra who has a smile on his face as he stares at Ian in adoration. Ezra takes a seat on the floor next to us, leaning into my side as he watches us.

Ian glances at Ezra curiously. "I'm your mama's friend," Ezra tells him softly, sending me a glance that makes my heart melt.

"Mama's fwend?" He says out loud to himself and then smiles. "Mama's fwend!" Ian climbs off of me and goes over to Ezra, who looks like a natural when he scoops Ian up in his arms. *Lord, help my ovaries.*

He could be such a great dad.

I watch in adoration as Ezra plays with Ian. They play with the blocks and cars that are on the ground. Every smile and giggle they share together makes my heart fill with happiness.

A smile never leaves my face while watching them. Annalise and Lee watch them bond from their seats on the couch. Ezra acts like a complete natural, grabbing Ian before he falls to the floor and comforting him after he trips over a few blocks.

"You're okay," Ezra holds Ian to his chest as he cries from being frightened.

He truly is going to be a wonderful father and that's all I can hope for.

Chapter Thirty-One

EZRA KINGSTON

L AYING IN BED, MY thoughts start to drift to Athena and Ian. I'm so proud of her. She is such a great mother and a strong person. It makes her ten times more attractive in my eyes.

When I met her son for the first time, I was pretty scared and nervous. I thought that I would mess something up or accidentally hurt him. But when I heard him giggle and look at me curiously, my heart melted and I felt like protecting him. As soon as he walked over to me, I just felt like I had to reach out and hold him, protect him from every danger in the world.

When he started babbling on about different things, I couldn't help but kiss his head and I swear I heard Athena whisper 'aww' when I did.

I talked to my mom about me stepping into the father role for Ian and she supported me and said that I should do whatever makes me happy because I deserve it. I'm going to tell Athena how I feel about her and about being a father to Ian. I want to be his father. I may not be his biological father and that's fine, but I would love to raise him as my own son. I want to wake up to Athena and him every day and fall asleep while reading him a book every night and do the things my father never did for me.

I snuggle into Athena's neck and close my eyes. "Hey, Sunshine," I mumble.

"Hey, Ezra," she mocks while running her fingers through my hair and I pinch her butt.

She shrieks and pulls on my hair harshly, making me wince and shiver. *Woah.* "Did you just pinch my ass?" She shouts while laughing.

I look at her and then smile innocently, "I don't know what you're talking about," I reply. *Yeah, smooth Ezra, smooth.*

I shrug and she punches my chest playfully. "That hurt," she whines and I smirk.

"Would you like me to kiss it better?" I ask, still smirking, making her glare at me.

"Do not tease me, Ezra Kingston!" She seethes while her blue eyes fill with salty tears.

I frown and pull her closer to me. She's on her period, so she's extra hormonal. I stroke her hair and pepper her face with kisses, making her giggle with a sniffle.

"I'm taking you on a date later," I tell her after laying there for a while and she nods against my chest.

"What should I wear?" She asks and sits on my stomach, straddling me, her legs on either side of my own.

I rest my hands on her waist. "Something like a dress," I mumble.

She nods slowly. "Yeah?"

"Yeah," I say and pout, making her lean down to kiss my lips softly. I kiss her neck harshly, emitting a moan from her and probably leaving a hickey.

Chapter Thirty-Two

ATHENA LEWIS

EZRA AND I ARE going on another date today and I'm pretty excited because he told me to wear something like a dress. It's been forever since I've worn a dress or something fancy.

I recently ordered some clothes from amazon and they came in earlier today. I ordered a dress, sweaters, new shoes, clothes for Ian and some black pants. I had a little money that I saved for myself from work and decided to reward myself and Ian. I think we deserve it.

Ezra left a little while ago to get ready and I'm now in my bathroom about to take a shower. I strip out of my clothes and step into the shower. I turn the water on and groan as the warm water hits my stomach, soothing my cramps. I'm on my period and I'm extra sensitive and bitchy.

I wash my hair with shampoo and conditioner and then wash my body. Turning the water off, I step out of the shower and wrap a fluffy blue towel around my body, and walk back towards my room.

I use the towel to dry myself off before I put on my bra and underwear. Placing the dress that I'm going to be wearing on my bed, I dry my soaking wet hair. The dress is light blue and it has ruffles at the top. It flows down at the bottom as well and I pair it with some white heeled boots.

After I get changed into the dress and shoes, I sit down at my desk to do my makeup. I do natural colors on my eyes and put mascara on my eyelashes, and then I put on light pink lipstick. Then, I start doing my hair and once I'm done with braiding it and putting it in pigtails, I pin them back and spray setting spray on my face, and check the time on my phone.

It's three forty-eight and Ezra is picking me up around four, so I finished just in time. I hate being late, but somehow I always end up being late for everything except school and work.

I get into Ezra's car and close the door, and look over at Ezra who is staring at me in adoration. "You look beautiful, but you don't need makeup. You're gorgeous without it," he compliments me and I blush.

"You don't look too bad yourself."

He's dressed in black jeans and a navy blue shirt. He looks absolutely hot, too hot for me and my hormones right now.

"Where are we going?" I ask as I watch the scenery around us blur.

"It's a secret," he mumbles. I pout and look at him, making him release chuckle. "Nope, I'm not telling you. It's a surprise."

I sigh in defeat and turn on the radio to occupy myself. I turn it up and start singing along while dancing in my seat. "Party in the USA!" I shout and Ezra does the same, me laughing when his voice cracks. He blushes and tells me to be quiet. I sober up from laughing and look at him with adoration as he drives.

Ezra pulls down a gravel path that leads into the woods. He stops in a clearing and I look at him. "Come on," he says with a smile on his face.

I get out of the car and follow him towards the trunk. He opens it and there is food, blankets, and pillows in the back. He lays the down blanket in the trunk and then lays the pillows down, creating a spot for us to watch the sunset.

I climb into the trunk and wait for him to climb in also. When he climbs in and lays down, I lay my head against his chest and grab some grapes out of the basket.

We eat some of the food and we watch as the sun slowly sets. "Ezra," I whisper, making him turn and look at me.

"I-I love you," I whisper, feeling like a weight has been lifted off of my chest. *What did I just do? Oh no.* I close my eyes, too scared to see his reaction.

"Athena, look at me," he whispers.

I slowly open my eyes and look at his face. He has a huge smile on his face and his eyes are sparkling with happiness, brighter than ever. "I love you too and I'm never leaving you," he says and then connects our lips. "I want to be a father to Ian."

I smile into the kiss. I love this man and that's never going to change, ever. He has me completely and I'm perfectly fine with that.

Epilogue

ATHENA LEWIS

IT'S HERE. IT'S FINALLY HERE. Graduation is today and I couldn't be any happier. Ezra and I are still going strong and are better than ever. I recently got custody of Ian and all of us moved into an apartment close to my mom's house.

Ezra has been bonding with his dad. His dad got out of treatment about a month ago and has been struggling with his sobriety. He's trying his best for himself, Ezra and Sylvia. He is still working on regaining Ezra and Sylvia's trust. I'm happy for him and I'm glad that he's doing better.

Spotting my mom holding Ian in her arms from my chair, I wave at her and Ian, who has gotten so big in the last couple of months. Just six months ago he was starting to walk and now I have to run to keep up with him.

When it's time, we all line up in alphabetic order and wait for our names to be called.

"Emily Colt," I clap with a smile on my face. I'm happy for her.

"Summer Fields," I clap and cheer for Summer, laughing when she blushes.

"Ezra Kingston," I cheer extra loud and people look at me like I'm crazy.

"That's my boyfriend!" I shout and Ezra shakes his head with a smile on his face.

"Athena Lewis," I walk up the stairs that lead to the stage and grab my diploma from our principal, and shake his hand.

"Yes, beautiful! That's my girlfriend!" Ezra shouts from his seat, making me laugh before walking off the stage, a faint and warm tint covering my cheeks. I walk back over to my metal chair and sit down.

"June Smith," I cheer and clap for her as well.

After all the names are called, we throw our hats up and cheer. I walk over to Ezra and his parents, who are talking to my mom, and I grab Ian from her with a smile.

Ezra wraps his arm around my waist and pulls me towards him. "Hi, honey," I say to Ian, who smiles at me with his thumb in his mouth.

"Hi, mama," he mumbles and then rubs his eyes, snuggling into my shoulder while looking around tiredly.

Ezra kisses my head. "You're gorgeous," he mumbles in my ear and I kiss his cheek.

"And you're handsome," I mumble back. He kisses my lips and I lay my head on his chest while we wait for our parents to stop talking.

"Dada," Ian whines and I hand him to Ezra, who smiles appreciatively, making me roll my eyes.

Ezra thinks that Ian is going to be a daddy's boy, but that's totally not happening. He's my baby boy and he always will be.

I lean into Ezra and watch as people filter out of the gym, waving back at Emily when she waves at me from across the gym. We aren't best friends but we are civil with each other and that's how I like it.

Ezra and I sigh in exhaustion, holding onto each other like monkeys. We just put Ian to bed and now we are cuddling. We lay there in the quiet room, enjoying each other's company while the fan blows on us.

I'm finally happy with how things are going in my life. I have a wonderful boyfriend that I want to spend the rest of my days with, a wonderful son who keeps me laughing at the stupid shit he does and amazing friends and parents.

A Few Months Later

"Hey, baby, can you hand me the tape?" I ask Ezra while I'm sitting on the floor, putting together cardboard boxes, my hair in a bun while I'm dressed in a sports bra and shorts.

"Here," he gives me the tape and then places a quick kiss on my lips. "God, you're so beautiful," he looks me in my eyes before grabbing my books and putting them in a box. I bite my lips as his back muscles flex. Ezra is shirtless and in shorts, and to keep myself from jumping his bones, I look away. *I would love to dig my nails into his back.*

"Thanks, handsome," I wink at him before standing up, my knees cracking as I stretch. Standing behind Ezra, I wrap my arms around his front and place a kiss on his shoulder

"Knock knock," my mom opens our bedroom door with Ian in her arms, chocolate ice cream on his face. "Almost done?"

"Almost," I grab Ian from her and wipe his face with a tissue that I grabbed from my box of tissues that sits on my bedside table. "How was your day, Mister?"

"Good," he giggles, laying his head on my shoulder while watching his father pack more of the boxes.

"How long is the drive?" My mother asks, leaning against the doorway.

"Thirty-Eight hours, but we're not going straight there," I tell her. Ezra applied to Penn State University and he got in, and I'm going with him as his girlfriend. It's a long drive from Seattle to Pennsylvania.

"He's going to throw a fit," she points at Ian.

"We know, mom," I laugh.

We can't wait.

Note to self, don't drive thirty-eight hours with a one-year-old. Throughout the drive to Pennsylvania with stops at hotels, Ian whined and cried a total of twelve times. By the time we arrived at our apartment, Ezra and I had raging headaches.

"Goodnight, mama." I close the door of Ian's bedroom and walk to the living room, sitting on the couch with Ezra.

"To a new chapter in our lives," he hands me a can of Dr. Pepper.

"To a new chapter," our cans clank together and we both take a sip, sealing the toast with a kiss after swallowing our pop.

About the Author

Alyssa DiSanza is a teenager in high school from Wickliffe, Ohio, a small suburb of Cleveland. Alyssa lives at home with her family and cat, Jack. She started writing at thirteen and now it has become a passion for her. When she's not writing or reading, she's usually hanging out with a few friends, painting or listening to music. Alyssa hopes that through her writing, she'll be able to help people escape reality and dive into the wonderful world of fiction.

www.ingramcontent.com/pod-product-compliance
Lightning Source LLC
LaVergne TN
LVHW041845070526
838199LV00045BA/1439